FIGHTING FOR THEIR MATE

INTERSTELLAR BRIDES® PROGRAM: BOOK 12

GRACE GOODWIN

GET A FREE BOOK!

JOIN MY MAILING LIST TO BE THE FIRST TO KNOW OF NEW
RELEASES, FREE BOOKS, SPECIAL PRICES AND OTHER
AUTHOR GIVEAWAYS.

http://freescifiromance.com

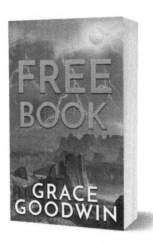

INTERSTELLAR BRIDES® PROGRAM

YOUR mate is out there. Take the test today and discover your perfect match. Are you ready for a sexy alien mate (or two)?

VOLUNTEER NOW!

interstellarbridesprogram.com

1

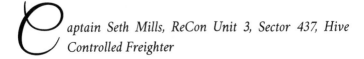

aptain Seth Mills, ReCon Unit 3, Sector 437, Hive Controlled Freighter

SMOKE CLOUDED THE AIR AS MY TEAM SWARMED THE TIGHT hallways of the small freighter, setting explosive charges. The Hive had maintained control of the vessel for the last eighteen hours. Too long by Coalition standards, which meant I had to get my team in, save the Prillon warriors pinned down in the engine room, and blow this fucking ship into so many pieces the Hive had no hope of ever putting her back together.

"Seems like a waste, sir." The man next to me, Jack Watts, was a former SEAL with a southern accent that only confirmed he was from Atlanta. Other than the fact that we were both from Earth, we had nothing in common. I was Army, six-four, two-twenty, and had no tolerance for bullshit. Which was one of the reasons Commander Karter had given me command of this unit.

Jack, on the other hand, was Navy, five years younger, and still had the bright shine of excitement in his eyes when we were on a mission.

But then, he hadn't lost two brothers out here to these Hive fuckers either.

"Shut up and set the charges, Watts," I all but growled. "You know the rules."

He placed an explosive on the wall next to us and pushed the button, activating it. "I know, but it seems a waste to blow up all these ships just because the Hive squatted here for a few hours. It's our damn ship."

"Not anymore." Three hours was the ReCon deadline. Eliminate all Hive on board within three hours or the ship was considered contaminated. Too dangerous to resume service in the Coalition Fleet. We moved on, farther down the hazy corridor with two of the unit on point, scouting ahead, and the rest following behind, checking the charges and watching our six.

"You humans stop chatting and get your asses down here. We've got a situation." The rough voice of a Prillon warrior I knew well came through the Coalition channel in our helmets. Along with the sounds of warriors yelling, ion blaster fire, and shouts to *hold the door.*

I picked up my pace. "Dorian. It's Mills. What's going on down there?"

"Hive blew the door. We're holding, but they hit half of us already. We won't last long."

"How many?" I started to run, my team falling in line at the urgency we could all hear in the pilot's voice. Dorian Kanakor was a big, golden son-of-a-bitch and one of the best pilots in our sector. He had a cousin and a brother in Battlegroup Karter as well, all three of them like giant lions when they entered a room. Golden hair, golden skin and yellow eyes, and the eldest, Dorian's brother Xanthe, with a permanent scowl on his face.

"At least twelve. Probably more. Double that transported in, but we took out at least six and the rest went to the control deck." Where they could alter the ship's course and upload Hive contaminated programming into the ship's systems.

"Fuck." That was Jack, and I didn't have the heart to chastise him because I felt the exact same way.

"Soldiers or Scouts?" I asked.

"Soldiers and..." The long pause made me nervous and I blinked the sting of sweat out of my eyes.

"And?"

"They have an Atlan. Well, what's left of one."

That just wasn't fucking possible. My entire team froze in place for a heartbeat, two. We were all dead if what he said was true. "Is he in beast mode?"

"Not yet."

"Roger that." I didn't know if the Earth slang would translate well or not, nor did I care as I turned to my team. "Set the charges now. Ten minutes."

No one argued. We either got through to the Prillon crew or we didn't. But either way, a captured Atlan beast turned Hive? He had to die. This ship, and everyone on it, must be destroyed.

I met and held the gaze of every man and the one woman on my team. Counted them off one by one, waited for their nod. When I hit my own detonator—the only remote one that would set off the entire interconnected set—the clock would start ticking.

Closing my eyes, I took a deep breath, opened them

3

and used my gaze to select the proper command in my visor display. A tap on my wrist activated the countdown, the numbers popping up in red in the corner of everyone's display. A countdown.

"Check your weapons. Everything on max. I don't care if we blow a hole in the side of this fucking ship. The Hive aren't getting off." I yelled the orders and moved at a run once again, racing to confront our enemies, feeding my unit the plan as we hustled. "I'm going in low, on the left, with Jack. Two men on the right. I'll throw the DPG and then we open fire, pull back. The rest of you hold back until we draw them down to the first turn in the corridor. We'll lure them away from the Prillon crew and pick them off in the smaller side corridor."

Beside me, Jack's face was grim. "And if he goes beast?"

Jack knew the answer to his own question, but our entire unit needed to hear it. "We keep the integrated Atlan busy until the charges blow. Whatever happens, no one gets past us. Are we clear?" The experimental DPG, Disruption Prototype Grenade, was so new, we would be the first to use it. The Coalition Intelligence Core had gotten their hands on some new Hive tech, tech my friend Meghan had taken from the skull of a blue freak in a cave during the battle on Latiri 4. I didn't know much, and she couldn't tell me more, but I was willing to try anything to get my soldiers off this ship alive.

"Crystal." That smoky, sultry voice belonged to Trinity, the only woman on my team, a hardworking, hard-playing Brit from somewhere around London. She'd been with me for two months and I didn't know her story. I didn't bother to learn their stories anymore. I'd lost so many soldiers to the fucking Hive, learning the details just made it hurt more when they died. Near as I could figure, I lost about a third of the team every few months.

The odds of going home were pretty much zero, and we all knew it. How I'd survived for so long, I would never understand. The other ReCon teams had started calling me Nine, as in nine lives, like a cat. I knew the truth. I'd been lucky. When the Hive took me the first time, my sister, Sarah, and her beast had come for me and dragged me out of hell. After that, I'd been more cautious, more meticulous in my planning. But nothing I did saved everyone. They all thought I was a lucky charm. Everyone wanted to be on ReCon 3.

"You're out of time, Mills." Captain Dorian's voice was harsh and a roar reverberated through the corridor with such force that the vibrations passed through my chest like a clap of thunder.

"Holy shit." That was Trinity, and she spoke for all of us. The Atlan had gone beast. A cyborg enhanced, Hive controlled, beast.

"Keep your shit together, people. Ion blasters will take him down. We'll take them all down."

"Not without dying, we won't," Trinity said.

"We're all going to fucking die anyway, Trin. So shut the fuck up and do your job." That was Jack, my second-in-command, and that hardcore order was the reason. "Unless you want that beast getting back to the Karter and taking out the whole goddamned world."

Battlegroup Karter was a collection of ten military and civilian ships holding this sector of space from Hive advancement. More than five thousand warriors plus civilian support staff, mates and children lived under Commander Karter's protection. And we served Karter.

"These bastards aren't getting anywhere near the Karter." We spoke specifically of the main battleship where we were stationed, but the nickname covered the entire group. My voice was a snarl but it calmed everyone down just in time.

Another roar.

One more turn. Thirty steps. Maybe less.

I motioned the bulk of my team to stay back and ran forward with Jack and two others on my right. DPG in my left hand, blaster rifle in my right.

"Low." I yelled as I slid down onto one knee and threw the DPG. "Fire in the hole!"

The Prillon warriors were close enough that I heard them shout and take cover. The Hive...I had no idea what the Hive did because my men and I were crouched on the other side of the turn, ears covered. Waiting for a blast that never came.

"One-one-thousand. Two-one-thousand. Three-one-thousand." Jack counted out as we waited.

Nothing.

"Well, we can officially tell the IC that was a bloody dud," Trinity's clipped British accent was icing on the cake.

Swinging around with my rifle, I took a look. The Hive were doubled over in silent screams, hands covering their ears. Two vomited, several stumbled into one another. They were disoriented and scrambling, confused. The DPG was working...on the Hive.

Except the beast wasn't affected. He stood, hands in fists at his sides, staring me straight in the eye. Shaking. He was shaking, but not reacting as the other Hive were. I couldn't explain the way the DPG worked and I didn't want to take the time now to figure it out. But, it was obvious it was set up to fuck with those fully integrated and the beast's response proved there was still some Atlan left.

Jack peeked around behind me and yelled for the others. "Take them all out. Now. Shoot to kill. Open fire."

The rest of the unit raced up the corridor behind us and it was like shooting fish in a barrel. The beast took a hit to his shoulder. His leg. His hip. The rest of the Hive Soldiers, mostly Prillon warriors converted by their evil Integration Units into Hive servants, were going down easy. But not the beast. Killing an Atlan in beast mode was difficult, but I'd never seen one take so many direct hits and stay on his feet. Hell, he acted like we were shooting paint balls at him.

I didn't want to kill the beast, but I had no doubt, if he were in his right mind, he'd prefer death to the condition he was in now. I'd been a Hive prisoner, faced the possibility of being turned into a mindless drone. The reality was beyond terrifying. I had fought alongside enough of the other alien races to know their warriors felt the exact same way I did.

Even my sister's mate, the Atlan Warlord Dax, had spoken of it on many occasions. No one wanted to end up covered in Hive tech, mind not his own.

It was a fate worse than death. And this poor Atlan? He needed to die for his own good.

"Hit them all. Trinity, you're with me. Focus your fire on the beast. We need to take him out."

The Hive Soldiers were falling fast. It took three or four shots to take them down, but they were still frozen, paralyzed by the new experimental weapon vibrating at their feet with a strange, high-pitched whine, like the buzz coming off high voltage electrical wires. My team and the Prillons inside the other room fired without mercy. Some of these Soldiers were once Prillon warriors, or Trion, or human. Hell, I had no idea where they were from. Some had oddities that I assumed had come from halfway across the galaxy, in a world I'd never seen or heard of.

We all knew death was better than being a Hive. Not only was the existence hell, but we would be turned into killing machines. Killing Coalition fighters, those we'd fought beside until the Hive took over.

And a mindless beast could destroy entire ships. There was a reason they built containment cells on their home world. Executed unmated beasts after a certain age. They were one-man wrecking crews.

I shot the beast, dead center in the chest. A merciful kill shot to his heart. He barely swayed.

"Jesus, what did they do to him?" Jack came up on my left, Trinity on my right and we all aimed at the beast just as he lifted his huge hands and removed his helmet. Most of his face was covered in silver, but there were pieces of him showing through. Dark eyes. Not silver.

I lifted my rifle for a headshot and his gaze locked with mine. Sane. Himself. Desperate. Hands at his sides, he dropped the helmet on the floor and waited for me to kill him. What the hell?

I hesitated.

"Kill me, Mills." The deep voice rumbled, but not with threat. It was a plea. And how the hell did this Atlan know my name?

"Do it now. I am Warlord Anghar. Kill me."

"Shit. Angh?" My body turned to stone. This was Warlord Nyko's friend. Nyko's best friend and commander. I'd served with him for two years and hadn't known he'd been taken by the Hive. Fuck. Shit. "Damn it. Hold your fire."

I glanced to Trinity and Jack, the raw pain I saw in Trinity's eyes a shock. Jack, however, looked at me like I had lost my damn mind.

"As soon as that signal goes down, he's going to be gone. You know that." Jack grimaced, his rifle still aimed. Steady.

"I know. But he's in there."

"Don't you shoot him, Jack. Don't you fucking dare." Trinity lowered her rifle to the side and shot one of the remaining Hive Soldiers standing behind the beast. We'd wiped them out. Almost all of them.

The beast stared and I stared back, searching my mind for answers. There had to be a way to save him. If Angh was in there, fighting against the Hive integration that took over almost all of him, then there was no way I could take him out. He deserved better. He deserved a chance at life.

The signal from the DPG faded and what was left of the Hive regained control.

Which wasn't much. Two Soldiers. It would have been nothing, an easy clean up, except for the beast.

With a roar, he turned and ran away from us, tearing through what was left of the doors so he could enter the room where the Prillon crew had been trapped.

"Take care of those two, retrieve the DPG and make sure the rest are dead," I ordered as I followed him in. Warlord Anghar. Christ. What a mess.

Our Prillon teammates hadn't wasted their resources. All around the edges of the room they'd set up barriers and defensible positions. But nothing was going to stop the beast.

"About time, Mills," Captain Dorian yelled, standing up to fire at the beast from behind a capsized table on my right.

The beast roared and advanced mindlessly, swinging his huge fists like wrecking balls. So much for his lucid moment. Whatever was left of Angh wasn't in there now. He was a drone. A servant of the Hive.

I knew the Atlan warlord was still inside him, somewhere. He'd shown himself. Briefly.

Everything had gone according to plan, everything except this. "Don't shoot." I held up my hand and gave the order as the rest of ReCon 3 flooded the room.

"The rest are dead," Jack reported and I nodded as the Prillon crew stood from their hidden positions and every single ion blaster and rifle in the room was pointed at the beast.

"Hold your fire," I ordered again, just to be clear.

"What the fuck are you doing, Mills?" Dorian bellowed at me as the beast advanced on him.

"Trust me." I caught my friend's eye. "Keep him occupied, but no head shots. Body shots won't kill him. Draw his attention. I need some time."

"You're insane, Mills." But the big golden Prillon warrior nodded and took a step back, firing at the enraged beast, careful to aim at his shoulders. His thighs. I had no doubt Dorian didn't realize it was Warlord Anghar. The beast's face was practically unrecognizable. Even then, I only knew Angh through Dax and Sarah. The

Prillon had probably never met the Atlan. The fighting teams rarely mixed on the battlefield.

"Whatever you're going to do, do it now," Dorian shouted at me as he fired again and again. The beast's body was singed, visible vapor rising from his shoulder into the air, but he kept walking. The Hive tech had turned a beast into a true monster. Stronger than any living creature I'd ever seen.

"Trinity, have the tranqs ready."

"How many?" she asked.

"All of them," I said. I meant to take Angh down, and take him home. "If he doesn't go down, take him out."

"You can't be serious," Jack grumbled, but Trinity was already reaching into her gear for the tranquilizers as Jack moved up to cover her.

I stepped back and grabbed the tranquilizer injections from her just as the beast reached Dorian. He wrapped his hands around Dorian's neck, lifted him off the ground like the seven-foot Prillon warrior weighed nothing, and threw him against the wall.

Dorian fell to the floor but was instantly on his feet in a crouch, blood dripping from his head, battle fury glazing his eyes. His battle cry was loud, a clear challenge meant to keep the beast's attention as I advanced on him from behind.

The distraction worked as the beast took a step forward to finish what he'd started.

I slung my rifle to the ground and dropped all my gear. I needed a running start and didn't want the extra weight. I ignored Jack's cursing and checked the angle of the injectors in my hand.

"Now!" Dorian's order was a boom in the room and I

ran as he reached for the beast, used every ounce of strength he possessed to hold Angh in place for precious seconds so I could make my attack.

Silently, I sprinted forward and jumped on the beast's back. The moment I made contact, I jammed the injectors into the side of the warlord's neck.

With a roar, the beast reached behind him, grabbed me by my armor and threw me so that my back hit the wall next to where Dorian had been moments ago. I slid to the ground in a heap and struggled to right myself, head spinning, the pain like I'd cracked open my skull. The iron scent of blood filled my helmet but I blinked it away as Trinity opened fire to keep the beast off me, shooting as his legs.

"Hold your fire!" I tried to yell, but the order came out more of a croak. I didn't need to worry. The beast swayed on his feet, fighting the drugs that flooded his system, but I'd given him enough to take down a large elephant. Even the Atlans weren't that strong.

Jack fired once. Twice. Like Trinity, keeping the strikes to the Hive implants on the beast's legs and shoulders until he toppled, unconscious.

Trinity lifted her helmet and looked at me, a slight shimmer in her eyes as she stared at the felled Atlan. "Why did you do that, Seth? Why did you have us save him?"

"Because he's my friend." One of the few still alive, if being implanted with Hive technology could be considered living. But at least now he'd have a chance. The docs could remove most of the tech and send him to live on The Colony. He'd never fight again, but at least he'd survive.

He might hate me for it. I knew that on a gut level. But I'd seen too much death. He'd just have to fucking get over it. Get tested for a mate, like my sister, Sarah, had talked me into last year. In a moment of weakness, full of whiskey and reminiscing about home, I'd given in and let her take me to the testing center for her Christmas present. She was so in love with her matched mate, Warlord Dax, that I simply couldn't tell her no. She'd risked everything to save my life. Denying her was not an option.

The testing? Yeah, that had been a huge mistake. First, it had been a year since I'd sat in that stupid chair and still no match. Second, I doubted I'd survive until the end of my tour long enough to get one. And if I did get matched before my service was up, leaving a grieving widow was not something I wanted to do. A pregnant wife? A child? No fucking way. Because if I had a mate, I'd want it all, but that was impossible. That was beyond cruel. I couldn't be that selfish.

Sarah didn't understand. She lived a different life. Warlord Dax had retired once they were mated and the two of them settled into civilian life on Atlan. They were wealthy, living in a massive home with servants and accolades for his time in the Coalition Fleet. They hosted dinner parties and played with their daughter. A different life and not one I could offer any woman.

Dorian crouched down next to me and I lifted my gaze to meet his. "You are one crazy bastard, Mills."

I couldn't help it, I grinned. It wasn't the first time Dorian had said those exact words to me, and I doubted it would be the last.

"Thanks for saving my life. And what's left of my crew.

How long do we have before my ship explodes?" Dorian asked, wiping his brow.

I glanced at the countdown in my helmet's visor. "Two minutes."

He grinned back at me. "Plenty of time."

Moving in teams, we rushed to the emergency evacuation shuttle, six Prillon warriors carrying the unconscious Atlan between them. The transport rooms would be crawling with Hive and we didn't have time for another fight.

Dorian threw himself into the pilot chair and I stood behind him as Trinity took the seat to his right. She was a flyer. I wasn't.

The two went through their checks in seconds and my knees buckled for a moment as the shuttle detached from the freighter. The shift caused anyone not strapped in to lose their balance.

"Clear?" Dorian asked.

"Clear," Trinity confirmed, her hands moving over the controls with practiced skill. I was too tired to even try to follow her actions. The shuttle lurched forward as the blast caused by the freighter exploding hit us from the side, throwing me into the control panel behind Dorian.

Alarms sounded from the wall to my left and Dorian reached back with an irritated flick of his wrist. "Don't touch anything, Mills."

"Shut up and drive," I grumbled back.

He chuckled and Trinity's shoulders relaxed, the tension in the air draining away as we moved farther and farther from the wrecked remains of the Hive occupied freighter.

When we were back in safe space, within the

protection zone offered by Battlegroup Karter's patrols, Trinity reached for the communication panel. "This is ReCon 3 for the Karter."

"Battleship Karter. Status ReCon 3."

Trinity looked at Dorian, who sighed. "We lost eight crew and all the cargo on the freighter."

"Seven survivors?" She was right, and she knew it. Hell, it wasn't hard to count that high. I'd been surprised that seven had held out as long as they did.

When Dorian nodded, she relayed the information to the control deck on the Battleship Karter. No doubt, Commander Karter himself was listening over the communication officer's shoulders.

"This is Commander Karter."

Hearing his voice had me rolling my eyes. Yup, he was listening.

"I'd like to know the status of Captain Seth Mills."

Trinity looked up at me, shocked. That was a first, Karter asking after a specific member of the crew. I leaned forward and she nodded that I could go ahead and speak. "I'm here, Commander."

"Excellent." There was a shuffling sound and Commander Karter spoke again, but his voice was quiet, as if he was speaking to someone behind him. "Tell Earth to go ahead and initiate transport."

"Earth?" I asked.

"Your matched mate will arrive in a matter of hours, Captain. Congratulations." The commander sounded pleased, but my heart was like a lead weight in my chest as my body filled with dread. Oh shit. Battling a Hive integrated Atlan hadn't been as bad as this.

An Interstellar Bride.

From Earth.

"Send her back," I blurted.

Dorian turned in his seat and pulled off his helmet, his golden eyes huge with shock. "What the fuck are you talking about, Mills? A bride is a gift."

"Not for me." I looked at the control panel as if I could will the commander to obey me. "Send her back, sir. I can't accept a bride."

"That is not your choice to make, Captain." The commander's voice was hard now, all levity gone at my response to what any Prillon warrior would accept with great joy. "You have been tested and assigned a matched mate. Your bride will have thirty days to accept or reject you. The choice is out of your hands. Your mate has all the power now, Mills. I suggest you get back to the Karter and have your head examined. Dock 3."

"Yes, sir." Dorian responded half a second before the line went dead. He turned to Trinity. "Can you take us in?"

"Yes, sir."

"Do it." He stood and grabbed me by the arm and tugged me out of the cockpit area. "Mills, come with me."

2

hloe Phan, Interstellar Bride Processing Center, Miami

LIPS ROAMED OVER MY BELLY. MY BARE BELLY. A SOFT brushing and then a flick of the tongue. Heat swamped my senses and I felt the rough shock of whiskers as he turned his head, his breath fanning across my sweaty skin.

My fingers were tangled in his hair. When had I done that? I didn't remember sliding them through the silky strands. Tugging. Then again, I didn't remember a guy being on his knees before me, learning my taste, my feel.

"I can smell your desire."

My scent. Holy shit, his hands cupped my bare bottom and pulled me in so his mouth could go…there.

"Oh!" I cried. My vocabulary was gone. Why? Because he had a *very* skilled tongue.

"Step nice and wide for me, mate. I want access to this pussy of mine."

The growl was rough. Deep. Etched with sharp arousal.

Unlike guys I'd been with in the past who hadn't found my clit with a headlamp and a compass, he found it with laser precision, flicking over the swollen flesh ever so lightly. Just the slightest slide on the left, across the top and back and my head fell back in surrender.

I was wet. Eager. Empty.

Maybe he was a mind reader as well as a pussy-whisperer because a hand slid up the inside of my thigh and unerringly found my center, circled my entrance then slid two fingers inside.

"You're so tight," he growled.

I tangled my fingers in his hair, pulled him back into place. "Don't stop."

Yeah, that was me. Begging.

I felt him smile against my most sensitive flesh.

"She likes this."

I did. I liked it a whole heck of a lot, but I wasn't sure why he was speaking to me in third-person.

"I can see that."

A voice came from just over my shoulder as hands came around to cup my breasts. Hands not belonging to the guy eating me out. I knew this because *his* hands were still on my butt.

These new hands were big, tanned, with a smattering of dark hair on the backs. I could feel a hint of callouses on the palms as they lifted and learned the weight of my breasts.

"Yes." I arched my back. I'd never been with two guys before, but this felt right. Somehow, I knew they were mine. And not just one hot night after hitting the bar kind of mine. But *mine.* As in forever.

The thought made me cry out and I heard their soft laughter.

"Yes, mate?" The man's voice was at my ear. Gentle, but deep. Resonant with a hint of need and quite a bit of power. His hands mimicked that; his touch gentle, but the way his fingers were rolling and teasing my nipples, he liked control. Liked to dominate me, even with the slightest of motions.

And it worked. Yeah, my nipples were sensitive, always had been, but this guy knew exactly what he was doing.

Both of them did.

They quickly brought me to the brink of orgasm and they hadn't done much. But then, I didn't seem to be in control of my body. Or my mouth as I begged them to hurry, to take me. As I called them mate and told them I loved them.

And I did. The feeling welled up inside me like an explosion, so fierce and desperate I nearly choked on it.

Which made no sense, because they weren't mine. I couldn't even see their faces. And I hadn't had a date in… well, a while. And never with two…

"Two males are better than one, don't you think?" The man behind me spread his hand over my chest, holding me down as his partner pushed me harder, one finger sliding into my sensitive bottom as he fucked me with his fingers and sucked my clit like his personal toy.

Had the man behind me not been holding me down, I would have bucked and crawled away. Their attention was too much. Too intense. "I can't take it."

"Yes, you can." He pinched my nipple, hard, just as the

edge of orgasm had been about to rush through me. How he knew, I wasn't certain, but I could feel his quiet attention. His need. His deep pleasure at seeing me submit to them both.

It was like we were connected.

And the man between my legs? I felt his emotions somehow. Knew he was determined to make me writhe. Scream.

Beg.

Oh, God. I was in soooo much trouble here. I should be freaking out. But this body, this strange woman's body, succumbed to the bliss. Welcomed it. Was familiar with their particular brand of sensual play. She was coiled tighter than I'd ever been, the anticipation in her mind impossible to resist. She knew her orgasm was going to make her body explode, her toes curl, her mind float away. And she wanted it.

Which made me want it. So damned bad.

Which made no sense, because I had no idea where I was, but I felt safe and cherished and protected by two strangers. But they weren't strangers to this body I was in, to her. They were hers. Her *mates.*

The man behind me fanned the swirl of my ear with his hot breath, his tongue following. "Two mates."

"Four hands." His palms gave my swollen breasts a careful squeeze as his partner worked my pussy and my ass with one hand. His other was laid across my abdomen, holding me down. Trapping me between the two powerful warriors. A finger curled inside me, hitting a spot that had me shifting my hips. The hand on my abdomen firmly held me in place.

"Two mouths." I angled my head to the side as his lips

slid down my neck, lighting a fiery wake. Instead of the tongue flicking over my clit, a mouth, hot and wet, settled over me, licked, suctioned slightly like he was kissing me there. Worshipping my body. The sudden gentleness, the feeling of being loved, washed through my mind like the most powerful aphrodisiac and I coiled even tighter. Desperate for them. Both of them. "Oh my god!"

"Two cocks."

I felt the hard prod of one against my lower back. Thick and long. I felt a smear of wetness and I knew pre-cum oozed from the tip. He was as needy as I was.

"My balls ache with a need for me to sink into you."

The guy before me swiped his flattened tongue from where his finger was deep inside me and up and over my clit. "You'll feel how big I am. How hard you've made me. How crammed full you'll be."

I licked my lips as I clenched down on his finger. It wasn't enough. I wanted that cock. I wanted the one that prodded at my back. I wanted them both. I wanted to be stuffed so full I'd never be able to forget them. I wanted to be *dominated.* And I wanted to be the woman who gave them pleasure. Who took their cum, the woman they cherished, would die to protect. *Theirs.*

This was crazy. Insane! I was dreaming—it had to be a dream—about two men. I'd never been with two men, let alone one guy who made me this hot. This needy.

I'd had sex before, I wasn't a prude. But it had only released pent-up energy. A way to destress. I'd had a high-pressure job for years and sometimes a girl just needed to get off and her hand or vibrator just wouldn't do.

A big cock was what was needed.

While I'd had a few big cocks, none had the skill of

these two. And we hadn't even gotten to the penis-in-vagina part.

"But first, you'll come."

"I want you now," I ordered, knowing they'd deny me. Knowing they'd increase their attention, their sensual torment. I gasped as they continued their attentions.

"You're our mate. It is our job, our privilege, to pleasure you," the one behind me murmured, then pinched my nipples.

I gasped and the man between my legs growled. "Do that again. She just dripped all over my hand."

"Don't stop," I begged again when he stopped licking my pussy to speak.

My nipples were pinched again, but nothing more was said. In seconds, I was brought to climax and I screamed. My body shook and I had no idea where I was. They completely destroyed me until the only thing I knew was them. They were real. Hot. Surrounding me. Keeping me sane as I came back to myself.

My blood thickened, my skin bloomed with sweat, my ears tingled. Lights even danced before my eyes. That was one hell of an orgasm.

"We're not done, mate." The one who'd ruthlessly played my clit moved back and the one behind me shifted, pulling me up so that my bare back pressed to the hot skin on his chest. His solid, muscled, huge chest. He pulled me back and suddenly I was pressed to his lap, my soft thighs brushing the rock-hard length of his, his knees bent enough so that I felt the flared crown of his cock slide over my slick and sensitive folds from behind. I felt the solidness of his body, the heat from his skin. He was so much bigger than me and I knew that he could hurt me easily. But that was not his intention. His goal was to fuck me, to make me feel good. Mission accomplished, but not finished. "That was just to warm you up. To get you all wet and swollen, ready for our big cocks."

The tip slid in an inch, settled. God, he was big. I clenched and squeezed around him, adjusting to being stretched open.

"More?" he asked.

"More," I breathed, wiggling my hips, but the hold on my waist kept me from moving, from lowering myself onto his hard length like I wanted to. I wanted him deep. Stretching me. Fucking me like a wild thing. Out of control.

"Bossy, isn't she?" the one who'd licked my pussy said. He'd stood, but I still couldn't see his face. Dreams were strange, blocking out the features of the man who'd eaten me out, but didn't hide his naked body, his lean torso, the big cock that thrust toward me, eager to be inside. But I already had a cock in me, sliding in, retreating, going even deeper.

I reached for the huge cock in front of me, wrapped my fingers around the head and used my leverage on his sensitive organ to pull him toward me. Slowly, so I could take my time. Look. Lick my lips. Make him wait. Torment him the way he'd tormented me.

He chuckled and lifted a hand to trace the soft line of my jaw, my lower lip. "You won't get fucked, mate, until my cock is in that hot mouth."

Behind me, the other man froze, holding me in place, suspended in the air, half impaled. Desperate.

With a smile, I pulled the cock closer and leaned forward, closing my mouth around the tip.

"Thank the gods." The roar behind me made me smile in satisfaction as my mate thrust up, hard and fast, burying himself in my tight pussy as my other mate thrust his hips forward, pushing his length into my open mouth.

His taste exploded on my tongue, nothing I'd ever experienced before. But she had. This woman whose sexual fantasy I was somehow hijacking. He tasted divine. Like heat and musk and man, and I sucked him deep, playing with his balls as the man behind me fucked me, my breasts bouncing with the force of his thrusts.

The pleasure built in my mind. Mine. Theirs. It was strange and overwhelming and wonderful as we all shattered together, my pussy clamping down on one mate as my mouth sucked down on the other. Locking us together.

One.

Perfect.

Aftershocks rolled through me and the men's voices grew softer, whispering words of love. Praise. Worship. I wanted to drown in it. Roll around in it. No one had ever talked to me like that. So much love. Devotion. Trust.

I never wanted it to end. But the voices faded. The room drifted in my mind like a dream melting away. I tried to hold onto it, but it faded. Left me bereft. Alone.

Cold.

Wherever I was, it was freaking cold. My body, my *real* body, shivered underneath a very lightweight fabric.

I startled awake, stared up at the plain white ceiling. I was breathing hard as if I'd run the hundred-meter dash, my skin damp with sweat. And my pussy? It ached from being filled with cock.

With imaginary cock.

I blinked, realized I was in the testing chair at the Interstellar Brides Processing Center. The *testing.* That hadn't been a dream, *exactly.* But what was it? The warden said the Coalition had such advanced technology that they could look into my mind, see exactly what I needed in a mate. Not wanted. *Needed.*

Did I need two lovers? I'd never once considered it before. But, God, was it hot. Sexy. Sooo sexy.

My mother was probably rolling over in her grave. Again. I'd thought the same thing five years ago when I volunteered for the Coalition Fleet Intelligence Core.

Warden Egara moved around the table to stand before me, tablet in hand. She didn't look surprised by my abrupt awakening from the testing, nor my current condition. Sweat covered. Pussy swollen and aching—not that she knew about that. But panting. Wishing I was still out in space, or wherever that was, and not in this stupid exam room feeling like a science experiment strapped to a dentist's chair wearing a thin hospital gown.

"Was that supposed to happen? Did I fall asleep? Was that a dream?" I asked, licking my lips.

I was parched from screaming, but had I really done that? Or had I screamed in my dream with this severe, and very serious woman standing watch over me? I flushed hotly at the possibility.

"Yes. The technology assesses your deepest subconscious thoughts to discover your perfect match from available warrior candidates."

My deepest thoughts were to get it on with two men? I'd never done it. Sure, I'd thought about a threesome. What woman hadn't? Sandwiched between two hot guys? I'd be down with it, but so far in life, I'd barely been interested in keeping one boyfriend, let alone two. But if it would be like that dream? I was okay with it.

"During the testing, I read your file," she said. Her tone was crisp, professional. She was from Earth, but worked for the Coalition, at least the Brides branch of it. Her uniform was a dark rust color, unadorned and familiar.

"Four years in the Coalition Fleet. Impressive." She moved to prop her hip against the table in the middle of the small room. "I assume I'd be more impressed if most of your time in service wasn't sealed."

"I'm confused. I don't know what you're talking about." There it was. The standard answer popping out of my mouth on automatic pilot. I couldn't talk about any of it. Not with her. Not with anyone.

But I had to get back out into space. I was suffocating here. Drowning in the minutia of a nine-to-five job. Drab apartment. Bills. Bullshit television shows. Surrounded by people I had nothing in common with. Earth? This just didn't feel like home anymore. I wanted back in space and volunteering as a bride was how I was going to do it.

3

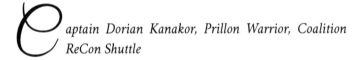

aptain Dorian Kanakor, Prillon Warrior, Coalition ReCon Shuttle

I GRABBED CAPTAIN SETH MILLS BY THE WRIST IN MY anger, but as I expected of a warrior, he pulled away and stepped close to confront me. He was nearly as tall as I, large for a human. And his strange blue eyes blazed with challenge.

And pain.

A pain I shared every day.

"What the fuck, Dorian?" Seth scowled at me, his voice carrying over the small number of warriors huddled around us. We were all sweat soaked and covered in grime from hours of battle on the freighter. But the room was almost silent as my crew and his ReCon team waited to see what was about to happen.

It wasn't often the commander himself connected with

us. Hell, it was even less often that one of us was assigned a bride.

"I need to speak with you, Mills. Alone." I toned down the irritation in my voice, knowing that any challenge would surely be met with resistance, not the level-headed cooperation I needed for this insane idea to work. An idea that had just come into my head after hearing the commander's news.

He studied me for mere seconds before turning to the co-pilot, a sassy Earth female named Trinity. "You get us back to the Karter." He turned, meeting the eyes of his second-in-command, another large human warrior I'd come to respect. "Jack, you've got the con."

I didn't wait for their agreement and my crew needed no such instruction, the chain of command as natural as breathing. Leaving their curious gazes behind, I led the way to the very small supply storage unit at the back of the shuttle. This escape vessel wasn't meant to hold many people. With all of ReCon 3 plus the survivors from my crew, the small ship neared capacity. But Seth followed me into the small space and I sat on a crate of emergency medical supplies. He sat opposite me as the door slid closed, sealing us in.

His calculating gaze leveled on me and he waited. Silent. Patient. I had no choice but to begin.

"My cousin, Orlinthe, was killed in battle a few months ago."

"I remember," Seth agreed. And he should. We'd all gotten drunk together more than once on the Karter over the last three years. When Orlinthe had been lost in battle to the Hive, ReCon 3 had been there, surrounding me and my fellow Prillon warriors, Earth whiskey in hand to drown the pain. Or at least burn it out of my throat.

"I was his second. I never tested for a mate of my own."

Seth froze in the act of wiping grime from the sleeve of his armor. A lost cause since all he did was smear it around, but it kept his gaze off mine. "So? Go down to medical. Do it."

"I don't want to."

He looked to me. Sighed. "Jesus, Dorian. You aliens don't make any sense. Why are we having this conversation?" Seth's head was tilted, impatience finally showing in the harsh line of his mouth and the tapping of his boot. He shifted on his seat, the butt of his ion rifle resting on the floor beside him, his grip on the barrel so tight his knuckles turned white.

"You have a mate, Seth. A matched mate. Do you know how special that is? How rare a gift?" I wanted to kick him now, wake him up. He was being a fool.

"Oh, no." Seth's eyes rolled back into his head and his chin rose at an odd angle before settling back into place, a strange smile on his face. Sometimes, human expressions were difficult to decipher, and I did not have the benefit of the psychic connection of a Prillon collar to help me understand. "Is this where you give me the lecture about how lucky I am? How I should get down on my knees and thank your gods for sending an innocent woman out into space to be my bride?"

"Yes." So he *did* understand.

"No."

"No?"

Seth stood and I did as well, the small space placing us nearly nose to nose as anger rose within me. How dare this warrior, this *human*, dishonor his matched mate? It simply wasn't done. "Why do you dishonor your bride?"

Seth barked with laughter, but there was no humor in the sound. Only pain. "I'm not dishonoring her. I'm *saving* her."

I frowned. "From what?"

"From me. From grief. From loving a man who could die tomorrow. I'm not ready to stop fighting. I can't go home, back to Earth. I'm different now. Too different for the mundane shit Earth people deal with every day." He sighed. "I can't have a mate. I won't do that to her."

"So you are a coward."

I thought, perhaps, the human would punch me for such a statement. But his shoulders slumped and he closed his eyes in defeat. Let his head drop so his chin touched his armored shirt. "I suppose I am. I won't leave a widow. Children with no father to protect them. If I accepted a mate, I'd be selfish, Dorian. I'd want it all. I'd want to fuck her until she had my baby in her. And then another. Pure and simple."

Yes, his desire was one most males shared, from all planets. I agreed with him, but I could see his problem. His *Earth* problem.

"If there was no danger to her, no chance that she would end up alone and unprotected, would you accept her?"

He looked at me as if I were crazy. "Of course, but that's—"

"Agreed," I said, cutting him off. "I will be your second. You are a warrior. You will claim your mate as a warrior should, with a second to ensure her pleasure, protection and happiness. She will be cherished by both of us, as a

Prillon bride would be. The risks you speak of would no longer be a concern. Should you die, I vow to care for our mate and protect our offspring. And I assure you—" I smiled then. "—she would be filled with that baby twice as fast if she belonged to both of us."

"What the hell are you saying?"

"You would need to make the same vow to me. That if something happened to me, you would be there for our mate and children."

That stunned Seth speechless, but I waited. He knew the ways of the Prillon warriors. He'd been in space long enough to know our custom. We always shared a bride to protect her from exactly what Seth feared. A Prillon bride was never alone, never abandoned. If one mate died, the other assured the care and protection of their mate and children. I very much had looked forward to sharing a mate with my cousin, but that was not to be. I respected Seth as a warrior. He was one of the few humans I counted a friend. And he'd saved my life more than once. I trusted him to care for a mate. To protect her, as I would.

But Seth was human, not Prillon. Humans, I had been told, were territorial, more like Atlan beasts than Prillon warriors. Perhaps the idea of sharing a mate was too difficult for him. There could be jealousy. Rivalry. Anger. Instead of making the closest of bonds with a shared bride, it would rip us apart. So I waited for him to consider my offer. I, too, knew the power of patience. Of silence.

When he raised his eyes to me, I saw hope, but also speculation. "And what if she refuses this arrangement? She was matched to me. A human. One man. She might not accept a second mate. Hell, she might be an uptight, puritanical freak who prays for forgiveness every time she has an orgasm."

I couldn't imagine such a female, but I had to assume there were some of such mind on Earth. Strange.

"Is this how you would describe your ideal match?" I asked.

"Hell, no."

I nodded, pacified. I doubted a warrior as strong as Seth would be attracted to such a female. And if that was not what he wished for in one, that would not be the match that had been made. "Accept her. I will be your second. And we will seduce her together. We will convince her that two mates are better than one."

Seth held out his hand in the odd way humans did to seal an agreement. "She will have final say. And if she doesn't want both of us, she goes home, or to someone else. I won't leave a widow behind crying over my grave."

I placed my hand in his. "Agreed. But unless you don't know how to bring a woman pleasure, I am not concerned with that possibility."

He scoffed at my obvious insult. "You talk a big game, Prillon. You don't know what Earth women are like."

"Enlighten me."

Seth shrugged. "Clingy. Needy. Soft. They don't like to get their hands dirty."

"I do not require my female to be dirty. I want her to need me and to be soft." My head buzzed with confusion. "Is this how you describe Trinity? Is she not an Earth female?"

Seth chuckled. "She's not a woman, she's a soldier, like my sister, Sarah. Soldiers are different. Hard. Tough.

They'll lead you around by the balls and run your life. I don't want that either."

"What do you want?" I asked.

"Hell if I know. If your subconscious bride matching system works like you aliens claim it does, I guess we're about to find out."

Indeed.

———

Chloe

"I don't suppose you can tell me what you were doing for the Coalition for the last four years? If possible, I'd like to place some basic information in your file for your mate. It will help him understand you and relate to your past."

"No, I don't suppose I can," I replied. I'd been back on Earth for a year. I'd served four years with the Intelligence Core. But in the last twelve months, I was rarely asked about my time with the Coalition. Not many on Earth believed in the Hive—especially since the news services didn't share any of the horrors the space bad guys were inflicting. As of now, Earth was insulated from the Hive by the rest of the Coalition planets. Even though there were some who volunteered to serve, like I had, the percentage was small. Earth met the volunteer quota required to retain Coalition protection and no more.

Earth's governments were still too busy fighting each other to dedicate serious resources to space.

And returning to Earth? No one who'd been *out there*

was allowed to talk about what they did. Even if the debriefing wasn't so severe, and we could talk, no one understood, or believed most of it. No one within the Emergency Services department in Houston believed me. I took 911 calls fifty hours a week and helped manage the worst-of-the-worst kinds of problems. Domestic abuse. School shootings. Hurricanes. Floods. Heart attacks. Car accidents. Humans would believe a story about ghosts or television psychics predicting the future of their love lives. But the Hive threat in space? Me, working undercover in outer space? Me, fighting aliens and infiltrating enemy lines? Yeah, my co-workers would have had a good laugh at my expense.

Not that I could tell them much. Just like some personnel within the US armed services, everything was kept confidential. SEALs couldn't say where they went on a deployment. Spouses couldn't be told a location. Missions were kept secret. Top secret.

Especially the new technology being developed to disrupt the Hive communications frequencies. And people like me, who had a knack for listening to their chatter and deciphering what they were saying. I couldn't explain how I did what I did, but I listened and sometimes the strange sounds just—clicked with my NPU in a unique way. There were others like me, but not many.

And one of them in particular, Bruvan, was wrong a lot. Too much. But he always managed to blame someone else. Blame the Hive for changing their plans.

Blame me.

He'd nearly gotten my entire team killed on the last mission, nearly killed me, and I'd been sent home, medical'd out, and he was out there still. Peddling his bullshit. Getting good warriors killed.

I had to bite my bottom lip to keep the anger in when the warden offered such a sympathetic ear. But I didn't know her clearance level, and I wasn't going to ask. "I really can't say anything about it."

The warden arched one dark brow and pursed her lips. "Well, it says you worked two deployments within the Intelligence Core, completing four years, before your return to Earth. You've been working as a 911 operator in your hometown. You've settled back into civilian life. Have a job. An apartment. Friends. And yet, you've decided to become a bride. Why?"

I frowned. "Does it matter? I'm here of my own free will."

Glancing down at my wrists, they were restrained to the arms of the utilitarian chair by thick metal bands. "Although, being strapped to this chair doesn't feel quite so voluntary."

She looked at her tablet, swiped her finger and the restraints retracted into the chair. "They are for your safety during testing and to protect me from those who have been convicted of crimes. Until the testing is complete, they've consented to the match, and they arrive on their new home world, they are still prisoners."

"Thanks." I rubbed my wrists, although they weren't chafed. The move made goosebumps rise on my skin as I became chilled in the hospital-style gown I wore. Breeze on the bare backside? Wouldn't want to miss that.

"You are far from a prisoner, Chloe. The opposite, most likely. I assume you have plenty of commendations on your record from the Coalition Fleet."

"Fishing," I said, forcing a smile from the woman.

"It's like that, is it?" She sighed. "You can at least tell me why you're volunteering."

I shrugged. "I've been to space. I know the Coalition, the type of guys who are qualified to be tested for an Interstellar Bride. I also know myself. I'm from Earth, but four years in space has changed me. Earth isn't the same anymore. I can't speak of what I did. Even if I could, no one would believe me. I'm just...bored. I don't belong here anymore."

"Go back to the Intelligence Core."

"I can't."

"Why not?" she asked.

I tilted my chin indicating her tablet. "It doesn't say on there I can't go back?"

She looked down and scanned farther, moving her finger over the tablet several times. Reading the fine print, I guess. I'd never seen my own file. "Ah yes. It says you suffered injuries that make you ineligible for service. But it doesn't say what those injuries were." She raised a brow, waiting for me to clue her in.

"I was hurt on my last mission. I healed eventually, but I don't want to ride a desk." That was all I could give her. It was the truth. There was no need to tell her that I wasn't allowed to return. They gave me the choice, retire or be forced out. They never expected me to want to go back.

I never expected to want to go back.

Maybe that head injury was worse than I thought. Maybe I was crazy for wanting to go back out into space. But, I wasn't going back. At least, not to the same life. I knew the odds, and there wasn't a chance I'd be matched and mated to Bruvan or anyone else I once worked with.

I didn't like them enough.

But who was I matched to? I'd interacted with most of the alien races. Atlan. Prillon. Trion. I'd only met one Hunter from Everis, but he was sexy as hell. Any of them would be fine with me. And with that matching dream, two lovers, I was pretty sure I was headed to Prillon Prime. I needed to know. The curiosity was killing me. "Was I matched?"

Warden Egara stood, went around the table, slid into the metal chair. "You have been matched. And it's a first for me."

"Oh?"

"You've been matched to a human. A man from Earth." She glanced at her tablet again. "It's a ninety-nine percent match."

I climbed from the chair, put my hands on my hips. "What? I'm not staying here." I was here being tested so I could leave this planet, not to end up stuck here.

She shook her head. "No. You won't stay here. You're matched to an Earth Coalition fighter. He's the captain of a ReCon Unit serving in a Coalition Battlegroup."

"What sector?" I was still reeling from something, my feelings a jumble about this. A man. A human man. I liked men—humans—just fine. But after that hot dream, I'd been hoping for two, huge Prillon hunks to totally blow my mind.

"437. Battlegroup Karter."

"Are you serious?" Sector 437 was a known hotbed of Hive activity. I'd heard of Battlegroup Karter. Some very high level tech had been taken from that sector. The first

Hive Nexus unit had been trapped there and eliminated by another human woman I'd served with in the Intelligence Core. Meghan Simmons. She'd been a friend, until she'd mated that Atlan Warlord, Nyko, and moved into civilian life on Atlan. I was happy for her, but I'd been alone out there with a whole lot of testosterone after she left.

And then the ship I was on blew up. Bruvan laid the blame at my feet. That had been fun, and earned me a trip home.

But I didn't belong here anymore. I felt like a stranger in my own town. I couldn't relate to anyone. I couldn't talk about what I'd done for the Coalition. I got up, went to work, fed the neighbor's cat. Day after day.

I thought of the dream that was quickly fading. Two guys. Not one. Definitely not human. No guy I'd met was that skilled. Or maybe I just hadn't met the right guy. "So, you're sure I'm not making a huge mistake?"

"Very sure. If you accept the match, you'll be transported to his location."

I began to pace and lifted my arm to tuck a strand of long black hair behind my ear. I got the dark locks from my Vietnamese grandmother and I wished with everything in me that she was still alive. That any of them were. But other than a few cousins I saw once or twice a decade, I was on my own. "What if I don't like him?"

"You have thirty days to decline the match and be reassigned."

"You sure I'm matched to a human?"

"Yes. Why do you ask?" Her brows rose with more than idle curiosity and I wondered just how much she knew about the kinky fantasies she'd sent into my head in that testing chair.

I thought about the dream. There were two men touching me. Making me melt and want and burn. But I'd never considered that before, so I could adapt. One man was enough. I could love one man just fine. My perfect match. A human. At least he wouldn't have tentacles or anything weird. Bulging bug eyes. A forked tongue. Scales. Claws. Ugh. I shivered. "Can he be sent back to Earth when he's done his service?"

"No."

"Why not?" I fired off the questions like bullets.

"Because no matched mates can live on Earth. Once he accepted the testing, he is no longer allowed to return to Earth, the same rule as you."

"Then we'll live on a space ship the rest of our lives?"

The warden sighed.

"Commander, sit down. Please."

She used my Coalition rank and that softened me. She saw me as someone from space more than just an Earth female. I did as she requested.

"Just like your time in service, not all answers are known. I *can* tell you this. Again. The testing is ninety-nine percent accurate. I can confidently say that you will be satisfied with your mate."

I thought of just how *satisfied* the men in the dream had made me. I thought of that for a moment, then a specific detail about what she said. "The only way you can be confident this works is because you've been to space."

She nodded.

"Yet you're back."

"I was matched to two Prillon warriors. They died in

battle. I chose to remain a citizen of Prillon Prime, but I serve the Coalition as a warden here on Earth. Someday, when I'm ready, I'll be matched again."

I felt for her. I could see the loss in her eyes, the pain of losing not just one mate, but two. Did testing other women to be brides fulfill her or make feel her loss even more keenly?

She didn't give me time to ask her these questions, for she stood, the chair scraping along the floor.

"State your name for the record."

"Chloe Phan."

"Are you currently married?"

"No."

"Do you have biological offspring? Or adopted children?"

"No."

"You have been assigned to a mate per testing protocols and will be transported off-planet, never to return to Earth. Is this correct?"

Never to return to Earth. Exactly what I wanted. "You mean I'll leave Earth behind and be transported to Battleship Karter?"

"Yes, Chloe. That is exactly what I mean."

I looked at the wall over her shoulder. I wanted off Earth. I wanted to fit in again. To be where I belonged and a battleship was very familiar to me. Maybe the testing was good.

What the hell. I'd find out soon enough.

"I accept."

Warden Egara looked down at her tablet, swiped her fingers. "Good. Hands back on the arm rests. Yes, thank you. Don't mind the restraints, they are required so you'll remain still for preparation and transport."

Preparation? Transport? I'd never transported in a chair before. Never in a hospital gown. I tested the restraints, but it was more practical than panic—like preparing for battle.

She swiped her screen again and to my shock, the chair slid toward the wall where a large opening appeared. The examination chair moved, as if on a track, right into the newly revealed space on the other side of the wall. The tiny room was small, and glowing with a series of bright blue lights. The chair lurched to a stop and a robotic arm with a large needle slid silently up to my neck but paused, one of the lights turning red.

"What?" The Warden was looking down at her screen with a frown, so I saved her a few minutes of confusion, telling her what I could.

"I don't need an NPU. I already have one—sort of." The thing implanted in my skull wasn't the standard issue NPU, but I wasn't allowed to tell her that either.

She lifted her gray eyes to mine, curiosity and calculation in her gaze. "And why, exactly, is it not showing up in my scanners?"

I shrugged. "I really couldn't say."

"Of course, not." She looked annoyed now, and I grinned at her to ease the sting. My NPU translated all the languages in the Coalition Fleet, just like everyone else's, but it was...more. Doctor Helion, the Intelligence Core's specialist on neural implants, told me the experimental Neural Processing Unit was coated in a specialized material meant to evade detection by Hive Integration Units in the event I was captured.

Thank God that had never happened.

"Fine, Ms. Phan. Good luck out there."

A sense of lethargy and contentment made my body go limp as I was lowered into a bath of warm blue liquid. I was so warm, so numb…

"Just relax, Chloe." Her finger touched the display in her hand and her voice drifted to me as if from far, far away. "Your processing will begin in three… two… one…"

orian, Battleship Karter, Transport Room

WHEN I WOKE UP THIS MORNING, I'D EXPECTED TO potentially die in battle fighting the Hive, not be claiming a mate. Holy fuck.

Yet the hairs on my body raised from the familiar electrical pull of the transporter signaling her arrival. *Her arrival.* I glanced at Seth, who, while completely calm of face, was holding onto his control by a thread. His hands were in fists by his sides. Not to punch someone, but perhaps the only outward way of showing his fear, his anxiousness, his worry at what a mate would mean, and what would become of her were he to be killed in battle.

After he explained to me why he never wanted that *damned Christmas gift*—his exact words—from his sister, Sarah, his nerves made a hell of a lot of sense. Completely paranoid, but reasonable, considering our duties in this war. Even more for Seth, for what he'd been through when he'd been captured and tortured by the Hive.

I hadn't been with him on the mission where he'd been taken, but I knew he'd been fucking lucky he hadn't been killed, or worse, *integrated*.

He was whole. Lucky. Completely free of any cyborg enhancements. But he hadn't seen it that way.

He saw it as a preview of the inevitable. He couldn't have a mate for fear of leaving her, or any children they made, alone and defenseless. His views were nearly identical to a Prillon warrior's despite the fact that Seth was from Earth, and had that planet's odd perspective on a proper warrior's mating. One male for a female. As Prillon, there were always two warriors for an Interstellar Bride. Two to protect, cherish, love and hell, fuck their mate into complete happiness.

I shifted my stance, my cock swelling at just the thought of claiming the female who was going to be mine. Mine and Seth's. A female to share between us.

And when I woke up this morning, I definitely hadn't thought I'd be getting a mate in bed, between me and my best friend. We were going to fuck her senseless, bring her so much pleasure she wouldn't remember what planet she came from.

Cocky? Gods, yes. I'd waited my whole life for a mate, never considered it possible after my cousin's death. I hadn't been tested, hadn't earned the right.

But Seth had been to hell and back. He'd earned a mate. Deserved one. *Needed* one.

"Incoming." The transport technician's voice broke through my thoughts.

Seth's spine stiffened.

The sizzle and hum of the transport came to a peak, then silenced as a female form materialized on the metal floor of the pad. She looked like an unconscious escapee from the med unit, her small body garbed in a familiar gown, but the wording repeated on it as a pattern was unfamiliar. English. Seth spoke English and while I could understand perfectly the language when he spoke, the NPU didn't work for the written word without a bit of practice.

Was she injured? Had she been hurt before transport? Seth rushed to her side, dropped to his knees before her.

"Call the med unit!" he shouted, not paying any attention to whether his command was being obeyed.

I was. With a narrowed gaze, I watched the two technicians closely to ensure a doctor would come immediately. This female was my mate and I wasn't risking anything, even a delay because someone was sloppy in their job, when it came to her. I hadn't even seen her face yet. Only that she was tiny in comparison to me. The thin gown covered her torso and down to her knees, but the slit in it—up the back—exposed the slim line of one thigh. Her skin was darker than Seth's, but lighter than my golden tone. Her hair was black as never-ending space and when Seth scooped her up into his arms, swung long down her back and over Seth's chest in a silky wave.

He stroked her hair back from her face as his gaze raked over every inch of her. "She's breathing."

I hadn't realized how tense I'd become until a pent-up breath escaped. My shoulders sagged with relief. Breathing meant she had a heartbeat. She wasn't dead. When she whimpered, a soft little sound, Seth groaned, pulled her in even closer to him.

I gave in and touched her, gently clasped her ankle, felt the heat of her skin, the softness of it. Felt the pulse in the valley between her small bones.

I met Seth's gaze and his expression was unlike any I'd ever seen before.

Awe.

Surprise.

Possessiveness.

Yeah, I recognized all of that because I felt it, too. Every single one of those emotions. But as a Prillon, I also felt pride in knowing Seth held our mate, that he would protect her with his life as I would with mine.

"Where the hell's the doctor?" I asked.

The technician paled and swallowed hard at my barked question.

"Sir, she's on her way."

"She's waking up," Seth said, his voice holding a tinge of hope and…amazement.

Shifting on my knees, I settled on her other side so while she was still on Seth's lap, she was between us.

Her eyes fluttered open and I felt a kick to the gut. It was like being hit by an ion blaster set to stun. Her big eyes were green. I'd only seen a few people with eyes that color, and definitely a trait of those from Earth. But with her black hair and medium-toned skin, they almost sparkled.

I watched her narrow throat work as she swallowed, as her pink tongue flicked out to lick her plump lower lip. All at once, she came to, surprising me—and Seth. She stiffened, sat upright, hitting the top of her head against Seth's chin. His jaw clacked shut and she scooted back, falling onto the hard floor.

"Easy," Seth soothed, holding his hands out, then sliding one up and down her arm.

"I'm fine," she said, her voice firm but soft. Everything about her was soft, small. Gentle. She looked...breakable.

How the hell was I not going to snap a bone or jar her teeth as I fucked her? I wasn't small, nor was I gentle. Carefully, I reached out and lifted her up, settled her somewhat awkwardly over my thighs since I was on my knees. I didn't want her on the hard floor. I wanted her wrapped in comfort. She deserved it.

Why? Because she was my mate. No other reason was needed.

"Yes, you're very much fine, but take a minute," I said. "You've come a long way."

She stilled then, her head turned to look at Seth.

While I didn't hear the transport room door open, I heard hasty footsteps before I saw the doctor's legs just before she squatted down beside us.

"You look well," she commented to our mate.

I'd met the doctor before. Atlan. Proficient. Efficient.

Our mate shifted out of my hold, used my arm to push herself up to standing. One hand grabbed the back of her odd gown to cover the gap in the material. Seth stood hastily and went around to stand behind her.

Good. Her bare skin wouldn't be seen by the transport techs. Not going to happen. If Seth hadn't blocked her modesty, I would have. Instead, I knelt before her, making the differences in our sizes so much more obvious. While Seth was human, he still hovered over her by a good foot. I knew I'd add another six inches to that and I didn't want her scared.

Not of me. *Never* of me.

"I'm fine," our mate repeated. "Just a little headache."

"Hmm," the doctor replied, studying her from head to toe with a capable and professional eye. "Let's start with the basics. What's your name?"

"Chloe Phan."

Chloe.

"Where are you from?"

"Earth. Texas." Chloe sighed. "Look, I just need a ReGen wand for the headache and I'll be fine. I always get one after I transport."

The doctor tilted her head to the side, but didn't comment. Seth did.

"You always get one after you transport? How many times have you done it?" He gripped the back of her gown and scrunched it up in his fist as he shifted to look her in the eye.

She shimmied her shoulders to work out of his hold, but reached back, took over keeping her sad garment closed. I wanted her in something that didn't look like a droopy sack. Hell, I wanted her in nothing at all—but only once we were back in Seth's quarters. *New mated* quarters.

Chloe looked thoughtful for a moment. "Too many to count."

The doctor was fiddling with the tablet in her hand, watching the display. "Spell Phan, please."

Chloe did.

The doctor froze.

"Is she sick?" I asked, noticing when the doctor stilled as she stared at her screen. My heart stilled, so did my breathing as I waited for the answer.

Instead of replying, she unhooked the ReGen wand from her belt and handed it over to our mate.

Chloe didn't fiddle with it as if it were a new thing for her. Instead, she flipped it on immediately, the blue light glowing as she waved it back and forth close to her head. She closed her eyes, let the wand do its work.

"Wait. What the hell is going on?" Seth asked, crossing his arms over his chest. "You've been to space before?"

"Yes."

"As a bride?"

She shook her head, keeping her eyes closed. "No. Not as a bride. Does it matter?"

"No." Seth and I both answered immediately and a small smile tipped up the corner of her lips. The thin lines of strain around her eyes and lips relaxed and she became, if possible, even more beautiful as she gave over to the healing warmth offered by the ReGen wand. I knew that feeling, the one where the pain just disappeared. Her voice, when she spoke, was softer, as if she were half asleep and my cock rose in response until her words registered.

"I was a Coalition fighter."

"I'll say," the doctor grumbled, then stood up from her crouch. "I'm not needed here. Remember, Chloe. You're not here with the Coalition but as a bride. Your mates will take good care of you."

She turned on her heel and walked out. What the fuck was the doctor talking about?

"Wait." Chloe's eyes snapped open and she dropped the hand holding the ReGen wand to her lap. "Mates?"

Seth grinned then. "You're matched to me. I'm Seth Mills." He tipped his chin in my direction. "And Dorian is my second."

She frowned, a little V forming in her delicate brow.

"You're from Earth. By your accent, I'd say American or Canadian."

"American. Born and bred, sweetheart." Seth grinned.

She turned her green eyes from Seth to me. "Yes, but Earth men don't usually share a woman. Unless you're into threesomes."

When Seth laughed, she looked back at him. "Only with Dorian." He stepped closer, brushed back the fall of her hair. "I'll only share you with him. But if you don't want both of us, say the word, sweetheart."

My heart stopped beating as Seth offered her an escape, from him. From me. I'd only been in her presence for a few minutes, but I already wanted to keep her. To fuck her. To protect her and claim her as my own. She was a dream, a warrior's fantasy, all soft curves and silken beauty. Her eyes darted from Seth to me and her breath sped, her pulse pounding at the base of her throat.

I stared, hiding nothing, not my lust nor my admiration of her beauty. I wanted her to know exactly what I offered. What we would demand. Surrender. Submission. Her heart. I would not be satisfied with less, and I knew Seth would be as relentless as I when it came to conquering our mate in every way. Body and soul.

I saw the moment her decision was made, the longing in her eyes seconds before her cheeks turned a pretty shade of pink. "Are you sure about this?" She asked me, but turned her attention back to Seth. "He's Prillon. You're human. If we do this, you can't change your mind later and go caveman if I want to jump his bones. Of if I fall in love with him, too. Or if I have a Prillon baby instead of a human one." She was listing off these possibilities as if they were sure, foregone conclusions.

That she would love me. Desire me. Want my child in her womb.

Every instinct I had roared at me to step forward and take her, fuck her now. Tell Seth to either claim her once and for all or get out of my way. But I knew our new mate was correct to question him. There would be no turning back from this, not for any of us. Once she was mine, Seth could not change his mind. He would have to kill me to tear me from our woman, and I had no doubt such an act would destroy her.

My friend turned from her to meet my gaze. Silent understanding passed between us. This moment was not much different than any other battle we'd fought together. Except this time, the prize was not survival, or the death of our enemies, but *her.*

Seth turned back to her and traced her bottom lip with his thumb. "I am very sure, Chloe. Dorian is a fierce and powerful warrior. I am honored that he would serve as your second. I can promise to give you everything I am, but that is all I can give. We can't stop fighting to protect our people. This way, you will be cherished and protected, in case…"

He couldn't finish the sentence, but he didn't have to. Chloe grabbed his hand and pressed his palm to her cheek. "I know. I know the risks." She released her grip on the ReGen wand and her free hand moved slightly, almost imperceptibly, closer to her side. I watched her fingertips tremble as she traced something beneath the gown as if it hurt her.

Chloe's green eyes were dark with mystery as she turned to me. "I assume you want this as well? To share me with a puny human man, not a mighty Prillon warrior?"

"Yes," I said, offering her a grin for the first time. *Puny?* "I have resigned myself to your Primary Mate's puny physical attributes." The laughter built within until I could not contain it. I had not laughed in months, not since my cousin's death.

Seth growled, leaning in close to whisper his words against her cheek. "I'm going to make you pay for that puny comment later. When you're naked."

To my shock, Chloe tossed her head back and laughed. "Bring it on, Captain."

Instantly, the mood lightened and she nipped at the tip of Seth's thumb when he protested again. My worry at her odd behavior evaporated. No, my mate wasn't hurt. She was sassy as hell and I couldn't wait to ride that fire, bury my cock inside the inferno I saw brewing behind her eyes.

"You're Seth's, that's for damn sure." Yes, even from the short few minutes I'd known her, she was a touch cocky and definitely bossy. Hell, if she really was a Coalition fighter, she'd damned well have to be. And Seth couldn't take his eyes off our mate. He claimed not to desire a female warrior, but Chloe already made a liar of him in that regard. He wanted her. So did I. "But you're mine, too."

Chloe took a deep breath, her mind working again with a rapid shift in her mood that fascinated me. She looked at Seth. "The warden said you are in ReCon?"

"Captain of ReCon 3, at your service." Seth grinned and reached out to take the ReGen wand from her lap. He turned it back on and waved it over her head. "All better?" he asked.

She nodded, but pursed her lips as if she didn't like him fussing over her. She chose to ignore him and looked at me. "And you, Dorian? What do you do around here?"

My name on her lips was like an electric jolt to my body. I wanted to hear it again. And again. "I am a pilot, my lady."

"Oh." Yeah, from the tone of that one word she knew what it meant for both of us. The implications. The dangers.

"No wonder you're so worried," she replied. "Adrenaline junkies, huh?"

I wasn't sure what the term meant, but Seth's shoulders stiffened and I waited for him to answer our mate's odd question. "I don't know, Chloe. I just know I can't walk away from this fight. And neither can Dorian."

She nodded. "I understand. Trust me. I so get you."

"Then you know why I chose Dorian as my second? Why it has to be this way?"

I stood then to my full height and I watched as Chloe's head tipped back to keep her eyes on mine. "Yes," she repeated, licking her lips again.

"If you've been to space before, then you know how this works." I might be Seth's second, but that didn't mean I wouldn't follow Prillon custom. Glancing over my shoulder, I looked to the transport tech, who'd been watching the entire exchange with rapt attention. Brides did not arrive often. His presence here was a gift to him, and he honored that fact well. "Do you have what I requested?"

He perked up and came around his work station. "Yes, Captain."

He held my collars out to me and I took them, the

three black ribbons of a Prillon mating. They were as familiar to me as my own hand. I'd had them since I came of age, waiting for just this moment, when I could present them to my mate. While I was the second here, and should have ceded to the primary mate's collars, Seth had none. He wasn't Prillon. But while Chloe was matched to him, not me, she was mine just as much as she was Seth's.

I wasn't willing to give up the deep emotional connection other mates shared through their collars. I'd been waiting for her. For this moment. If Seth didn't like it, he could choose not to join us in our psychic bond. But Chloe? She was mine. I needed to feel what she felt, to know when she was happy or frightened or aroused. She would wear my collar.

I thanked the tech and turned back to my mate and Seth.

"A Prillon mating collar," she murmured, eyeing me.

"It would be my honor, my privilege to wear a collar that matches yours. My collar will proclaim to all that you are under my protection. My mate. That I am yours. I am possessive, Chloe. I need to see my mark on your body, know that none would dare touch what was mine. Will you honor me and accept the collar?"

"What about you?" she asked Seth.

He flicked his gaze to mine. He knew what the collars represented, what they would mean to anyone who saw one around his neck. My neck. Hers. He also knew of the connection we would share with her. "Dorian?"

I held out a collar and Seth took it from my hand as I spoke. "The choice is yours. But I will not be denied. She is mine as much as she is yours."

Seth nodded. "Can't let you have all the fun, now can I?'

Chloe smiled, but Seth's serious expression caused her smile to wilt like a flower in the driest desert. "I will wear your collar, Chloe. From this moment, I am yours. You and I, we humans, don't have any kind of customs out here in space. There's no church, no priest, no one to marry us. Just know this, sweetheart, when I take you the first time, there's no going back. You'll be mine."

Her mouth fell open. "I have thirty days to decide, hotshot," she countered.

Seth gave a slight shrug. "Yes, by Coalition law. But that doesn't mean you won't be mine."

She frowned, seemingly not liking his bossy answer.

"The collar is black. When Seth and I claim you in the formal Prillon tradition, it will change to gold, my family's color."

She took a step back. "I know all about the Prillon mating ceremony and I'm not fucking you guys in public. Not happening." She crossed her arms over her chest and I could see the slight swells of her breasts plump up beneath the thin material of what looked like a hospital gown.

Seth didn't even look at me. "I'll share you with Dorian, sweetheart. No one else. As for the Prillon claiming custom, Dorian can have his collars. He won't have his way with the rest. No public fucking for you. Ever."

Her slight shoulders slumped in relief.

I was surprised by my own emotions in this. I'd known my whole life I'd fuck a mate with another male, that I'd claim her publicly. I'd been fine with that. Until now.

Just knowing that with her arms now crossed over her chest, the back of her gown was split open, baring her curves, had me wanting to toss her over my shoulder and carry her back to our private quarters. We'd requested the new quarters upon our return from the last mission, moved everything we both owned into the new suite in less than an hour.

We were warriors. The only thing that truly belonged to us, that mattered, was standing before us in this room. Chloe. She was ours and I used every ounce of self-control not to rush to her and explore every inch of her body with mouth and lips and tongue. My need was growing, and feral. Unexpectedly hard to control.

But then, I had not expected our mate to be so beautiful. So sassy. So soft and perfect.

The transport tech watched us all without blinking, his concentrated interest in our mate no longer feeling like a point of pride, but an annoyance. He looked at what was ours. *Wanted* what was ours.

No. I would not claim her publicly. This tiny Earth female was ours and no one else's. Her pleasure, her skin, her surrender? Ours and ours alone.

"No public claiming," I confirmed.

I lifted a collar to my neck, affixed it and felt the seam seal close, the material adjust in size to fit about my neck. A slight buzz coursed through my body, as if an open communications channel had been made, but there was no one else on the line.

Chloe looked to me, then to Seth, then back, studying the collar about my neck. After a minute, she put her hand out, palm up, but I stepped closer to her.

"Allow me, Lady Mills. Please." I addressed her by her

new, formal title for the first time and felt more than saw Seth shudder next to me at the finality of those words. Lady Mills. Claimed. Collared. Ours.

I raised the collar toward her neck. Seth came around behind her, lifted the long fall of her hair so I could encircle her slim nape. The sides of my hands brushed her soft skin. So warm, so smooth. The collar joined, then sealed and I moved my hands away to watch as the collar resized to her neck.

My cock pulsed at the sight of it about her neck, but when I felt the jolt of her emotions through my own collar, I gave a slight groan.

Seth looked to me and I watched Chloe's eyes widen. "Do you feel me, mate?" I asked.

She nodded and I staggered as her desire sliced through me like a blade made of pure flame. She wanted us, all right. She wanted us almost as much I wanted her.

Seth placed a chaste kiss on the back of her neck and her fluttered response moved through me like the fast, frenzied flight of a dozen tiny wings. Seth let her hair fall and stepped back to place the last collar on himself.

His possessive fire joined the swirl of emotions coursing through our mate and she swayed on her feet, licking her lips as her eyes glazed with desire. Need.

"You Prillons are geniuses, Dorian," he murmured, once his was fitted as well. His eyes locked like laser sights on our mate.

I could feel them both. Their emotions, their need. Not just Seth's toward Chloe—she was a beautiful female —but also hers for us.

"So, are we done here? I'd like to get out of the transport room." Chloe's hands fluttered nervously as she stared us down, accepted the powerful flood of my desire for her combined with Seth's. He was not Prillon, but his need for her, his protective and possessive feelings, were every bit as strong as my own, and I knew I had made the right choice, the only choice, in becoming his second.

Chloe. Beautiful Chloe, was ours. And now, with the collar about her neck, she knew exactly how much we wanted her.

"We're not done," Seth said, his voice almost a growl.

"Not even close," I added.

Chloe shook her head as if she were stunned by the feelings swirling between us. It was potent. Intense.

There would be no escape, for any of us.

I swept her into my arms, unable to fight the need to touch her for another moment. Seth didn't argue, feeling my need to possess her, simply led the way to our quarters. It was time to make Chloe ours.

5

eth

I LED THE WAY TO OUR NEW PRIVATE QUARTERS, THE SPACE I'd be sharing with both the Prillon warrior and Chloe, our mate.

Mate. Just a few days ago, that word lay heavy on my heart. All I could see was loss and pain and longing for something that could never be. I was human. I was ReCon. My team joked that I had nine lives, but I knew the truth with a bone deep certainty. I only had one.

And now it belonged to her.

As meticulous as I'd been in my planning before, as much as I did to protect my team, I vowed to redouble my efforts. No one was going to take me from Chloe without a fight. And if the unthinkable happened, I'd be at peace, knowing the massive, protective, over-bearing, smart-ass warrior carrying our mate down the hallway would protect her and cherish her to the last breath in his body.

I knew. Thanks to these damn collars. His need, his instinct to claim her, was riding him hard, testing my control. We were both so amped up at the prospect of fucking her, that I was having a hard time remembering where to turn in the maze of cream colored hallways.

Civilian living quarters.

Another first. Thanks to her.

After just a few minutes—that felt like hours—we arrived at the door. I stopped without opening it and turned to Dorian, and the tiny woman he held in his arms.

God, she was beautiful. Long black hair as smooth as silk. Almond shaped eyes that were a startling green against her creamy skin. Her eyes were large and she stared at me with a combination of emotions I would have had no hope of unraveling without the help of these genius Prillon collars. Hope. Nerves. Lust. Anxiety. Longing.

I looked up at my second. "Put her down, Dorian. We do have one custom on Earth that I need to keep."

Dorian shrugged and gently placed Chloe on her bare feet in the hallway. It was mid-morning, and everyone was either on duty or at work. The hallway was empty as I scooped Chloe into my arms and asked Dorian to open the door as I stood before it, cradling my new bride. There was no long, flowing gown, no diamond on her finger, but she was mine, and I would carry her over the threshold into our new life together.

The door slid open and I looked down into Chloe's upturned face. "You ready for this?"

She grinned up at me and her arms came up to wrap

around my neck. It was a picture-perfect moment happening billions of miles from home. No white picket fence. No dogs, or a floral bouquet, or any of the rest of the things humans associated with this moment. Just me. And her.

And an alien watching us like we were both out of our minds. "I assume this is some strange Earth custom?" Dorian asked.

"Yes." We both answered in unison.

"A man carries his bride across the threshold the first time she enters their new home," I explained.

"Why?"

Chloe smiled up at him. "I have no idea, but they do."

Dorian looked at both of us for a moment, then nodded his head as if making a serious decision. "Then, I will not be denied this custom."

Before I could react, he'd moved behind me and lifted both of us into the air. Chloe squealed and grabbed onto me, hanging on for dear life. I barked with laughter at Dorian's huff of exertion and cursing as he plodded through the open door.

"You are heavier than you look, human."

Chloe burst out laughing and the joy and excitement coming through her collar, the blast of fun and happiness silenced any protest I might have made at Dorian's odd gesture. Chloe was still laughing. "You two are going to be crazy, I can just tell."

She was still laughing when Dorian set me down on my feet. But Chloe remained in my arms. I couldn't bring myself to let her go.

The door slid closed behind us and Dorian walked to one side of the room, opening a drawer. I paid no attention to him, my entire being centered on the woman in my arms. It had been so long since I'd held something soft and pure and giving. She was love and laughter and light, I could feel the strength of her soul, her hope, bubbling up between us. And I was too weak to turn away, to lose contact, even for a moment after so many years of pain and horror and denying myself the comfort of a woman's arms out of fear that I'd somehow hurt her.

Or lose myself.

As I looked into Chloe's eyes, her smile faded and the intensity spiraled.

"I can't let you go."

She lifted a hand to my face. "I know. I can feel it. It's okay."

I leaned down and buried my face in her hair. She smelled like home. Like cinnamon sugar cookies and spring breezes and sunshine.

The room was a blur as I walked to the bed. I knew what was here. Dark blue couch and chairs. A small table meant for three. A bathing room and an S-Gen in the corner. Closets and drawers built into the walls.

And our bed. The biggest bed I'd ever seen. Dorian had acquired the standard size mating bed the Prillon used, and it was more than big enough for the three of us.

It, too, was draped in blue because Dorian had read Chloe's preferences and knew it was her favorite color.

The pillows were gold, his nod to his ancestry, the color our collars would become once Chloe was officially ours. He'd asked my opinion and I'd given him the truth. I didn't give a flying fuck what color anything was, as long as our mate was naked between the sheets.

And happy. The need to make her happy weighed on

me like an anchor and the old doubts, the old worries started to creep back into my mind as I sank down on the side of the bed with Chloe in my lap. I settled her there and wrapped my arms around her torso, pulling her closer, pressing her to me with as much gentleness as I could muster.

Which wasn't much. I trembled with the effort to hold back, to be gentle with her when the need within me was like a wild animal with sharp claws. "I can't let you go." I said it again, begging for forgiveness. I'd denied myself this dream, turned away from it and endured the pain and loneliness. Accepted a black, bitter, lonely death protecting Earth from an enemy so horrifying I had to keep being a fighter. I had to stop the Hive.

Having her here, in my arms, was like ripping open that old wound, releasing years of pent-up emotions like a tidal wave that was drowning me.

Drowning all three of us.

Dorian staggered and dropped to his knees just out of reach before me. Beside him, on the floor, was the one thing I'd forgotten about, the training box the Prillons used on new brides to ready them to accept two mates at once, one in the pussy and one in the ass.

The thought of fucking her with Dorian made my cock so hard my balls ached, increased my need. I never bothered to imagine that would be possible for me, but now? I wanted it. Wanted her spread wide, open and accepting of both our cocks. Begging for more. Completely mindless with pleasure as we both worshipped her body. A groan escaped me and Chloe wiggled in my arms. My vice-like grip tightened. If I moved, I'd lose control.

"Seth," she whispered my name, her voice like a soothing balm. There was no judgment there, just acceptance. And a need that rivaled my own. God bless the fucking collars. She knew. I didn't have to say anything.

I breathed deeply, my nose and lips pressed to her bare throat. "I want to know everything about you, Chloe. Everything. I need to know you. But right now..." How could I tell a woman I just met that I was on the edge of losing control, that the alien collar around my neck was making me insane with the lust of two powerful warriors, that if I moved at all, I might throw her down on the ground and rut into her like a crazed animal?

Dorian leaned forward, his hands in fists pressed to the floor as he, too, fought for control. "By the gods, Seth, you're going to drive us all mad."

I shook my head. I had a plan. I'd done nothing but think of how I would take her this first time. How we would talk to her, learn her, touch her slowly and build her need. I'd thought it through to the finest detail—where I would kiss her first, the words I would speak as I made her mine, the words I would give Dorian, my second, for making this possible for both of us. I owed him a great debt, for I would never have taken a bride alone.

When her fingers lifted and fisted in my hair, when she turned her head and her mouth found mine, my plans evaporated like dust in the wind. It seemed the collars worked for her as well.

"Kiss me. Fuck me. Rip off this stupid hospital gown and make me yours. I want you. I want you both. Now. Right now." Chloe's words detonated in my mind and before I could fight for an ounce of self-control, I ripped the gown from her body and claimed her mouth with my tongue and her hot, wet pussy with two fingers buried deep. I pumped into her, rubbing her clit hard and fast, without mercy, until she arched in my arms on a silent scream and her body pulsed, hot and tight, around my fingers.

One. That was one. And she hadn't screamed my name. Hadn't begged.

I was going to make her beg.

———

Chloe

Oh. My. God.

Seth's tongue invaded my mouth, demanding and relentlessly tasting. Exploring. Owning me in a kiss. His fingers pushed deep, no foreplay, no teasing, and I arched my hips into his rough touch, needing this. Needing more.

Behind me, I knew Dorian watched, listened, his presence and attention making me feel beautiful and sexy and oh-so-naughty. I loved knowing he was there, wanting to join in, watching us, devouring me with his eyes. I felt it through the collar. Where Seth was familiar and hot as hell in a very comforting way, Dorian was alien. Golden, like a lion. His hair and skin were beautiful. His features were sharper than a human's, his teeth a bit more pointed, his eyes? Amber, like a cat's, and intensely focused. His features were humanlike, but sharper, the angles of his nose and cheeks more distinct. Primitive and masculine in a way that made me feel very, very feminine. His raw lust pulsing through the collar added gasoline to an inferno and I broke, I shattered in seconds, my body not my own. I'd never come like that before. Not that easily or quickly. Or with such need.

Seth's hand stilled, pressed deep, holding me open and impaled on his thick fingers as he kissed me over and over, his hunger a drug that fed my own.

Throwing my arm out to the side, I tangled it in Dorian's long, golden hair and pulled him toward me, until his lips latched onto my nipple. Dorian growled, the sound shooting straight to my clit so that I cried out into Seth's mouth as he suckled me, his free hand moving to my thigh, pulling my leg wide, to the side, open for Seth's exploration.

Seth lifted his head from mine. "Taste her pussy, Dorian. Taste her. I want to know if she's sweet."

Dorian's answer was a groan and he popped my nipple free to trail his lips over my side. He lingered for a few seconds when he discovered my scar, the foot-long tribute to my past, and Bruvan's fuck-up, the mistakes I'd had to learn to live with. But he moved on quickly, pulling my leg wider and shifting me to settle it over his shoulder. My other leg remained on Seth's thigh, my bottom in mid-air as Dorian lowered his mouth to hover over my pussy. The wet pussy where Seth's fingers still stroked me deep, on the inside, driving me wild.

As soon as Dorian was in position, Seth's fingers slid up over my clit slowly, as he left me open for his second's mouth.

I thought Seth was lost in the moment, but I was

wrong, as his fingers trailed up my side, tracing the scar there, the scar that Dorian had paused to study for no more than a second.

His fingertips trailed over the wound lightly, a blast of protective pain coming through the collar, and I whimpered in response, tears threatening to overwhelm me as the emotional rollercoaster I was riding with these two plummeted and rose with a speed and fury I had trouble containing.

Seth continued his journey until that same hand was buried in my hair, holding me in place for the mastery of his kiss.

I melted. Completely under his spell.

And then Dorian's mouth clamped onto my pussy, tongue going deep, then sliding free to suck and tease my clit. I was spread between them, held in place, I had no choice but to submit. To surrender.

And the truth was, I didn't want them to stop. I needed this just as much as they did.

Dorian worked me to a second peak, my orgasm deeper, longer than the first frantic release. My toes curled and I could not stop the long, keening moan that drifted into the room as Dorian clamped down on my clit, sucking it into his mouth, two fingers buried in my pussy as I lost control once more.

Even before I came back to myself, Seth tore his mouth from mine. "Dorian, take off your clothes and pull her into your lap. Fuck her."

Dorian's lips trailed kisses over my inner thighs, his touch so gentle and reverent that I didn't think to be embarrassed or ashamed of my reaction to them. To both of them. How could I when I knew just how they felt, what they desired through the collars? Dorian shook his head, his nose gently brushing the soft, sensitive skin. "No, Seth. By the law of Prillon Prime, as her Primary Mate, it is your right to claim her first, to get her with child. I can't claim her pussy—"

"I'm not Prillon, Dorian," Seth countered. "I want to watch you fuck her. And that ass? I want to play while you do."

His words made Dorian shudder, but he didn't argue. He stood at my feet and removed every ounce of his clothing in seconds. I stared up at him, at his ripped abs and non-stop chest muscles. His shoulders were huge. His thighs powerful. His cock? God, my pussy clenched and I couldn't take my eyes from that hard, golden length. I wasn't sure I could take it all. Take him. Take them together.

But my body clenched in anticipation. Eager to try.

"Chloe. Mate. Look at me." Dorian stood, hands on his hips, watching me as I took him in, drank my fill of his gorgeous body.

I met his gaze and waited.

"I want to fuck you, Chloe. I am not your matched mate. I am your second, a second you didn't request. I need to know if this is truly what you want."

There was no hesitation in me as the dream I'd had in the testing center came back to me full force. Two men. Wanting me. Loving me. Protecting me. *Touching* me. "Yes. Dorian. I want you. I want both of you."

That fast, he pulled me from Seth's arms and crushed me to his chest. Lips found mine and he conquered my mouth with every bit as much fervor as Seth had. He was tall. Huge. My feet dangled around his knees as he held me suspended against his body. He was at least seven feet tall. Seth was big as well, probably six-four, but Dorian? He was huge. Shoulders. Chest. His hands covered nearly my entire back as I drowned in his kiss, tasted my desire on his lips.

He turned us, but I paid no attention until he sat and pulled my legs wide, to either side of his hips. I straddled him, the top of his huge cock pressed to the opening of my empty pussy, and I held myself there, poised above him, my hands tangled in his hair, head thrown back in blatant invitation. I wanted his mouth on me, sucking my nipples as I took him deep.

I didn't need to ask. He bent low, arching me back so that he supported my weight as his lips clamped down on one breast.

I reached down, around my bottom, twisting in his grasp to place his cock exactly where I wanted it. When I was sure he could not escape, I shifted. Took him in, inch by inch, his wide cock stretching me open with a burn that made me moan and wiggle, eager for more. I needed him deep. All the way. Stretching me wide. Filling me up.

Using my inner muscles to squeeze and relax, I worked myself down onto his hard shaft until he was fully seated. My ass pressed to his thighs. As deep as I could take him.

He released my breast from his mouth, threw his head back and growled, shifting on the bed, lifting his hips, driving even deeper.

I wrapped my hands around his neck and held on as he bucked beneath me, his body hard as a rock, his cock filling me to the brink of pain. When I thought sure he was going to lose control, he stopped, his hands landing on my ass, pulling my cheeks wide. He opened me up and I gasped as something warm and wet pressed to my back entrance.

"This ass is ours, Chloe. We're both going to take turns fucking you here. Your pussy. Your mouth. You're ours now." Seth knelt behind me, his rapt attention on my bottom as Dorian held me open for him. I turned my head to find a box filled with an assortment of anal plugs of various sizes at his side. He held a smaller one out for my inspection, his brows raised, a question in his eyes, even as his finger pressed inside that delicate place, spreading a warm, oily substance inside me. Getting me ready.

His finger worked slowly. Gently. Dorian's soft words rumbled through my ear where it rested against his chest. "Relax, mate. Let him in. Give us everything. We will take care of you." He petted me with his huge hands, running them up and down my back, his cock still buried deeply inside me. I was impressed he could hold himself still. If Seth weren't playing with my ass, I doubted I'd be able to remain still. My inner walls clenched and squeezed Dorian's cock.

I met Seth's eyes and nodded, before closing my eyes and turning to bury my face in Dorian's hard chest. Breathed him in. He smelled wild, like forest and wind and the fury of a thunderstorm. I couldn't define it, perhaps because he was not human, but his warmth and scent, his huge hands at my back made me feel safe. Protected.

Cherished.

Seth worked the plug inside me gently, breaching my tight hole with a soft pop that made me gasp and wiggle as my body adjusted to the invasion, the slight burn.

But then?

Fire.

I was too full. Dorian's cock suddenly even tighter in my wet, swollen core. I groaned as nerve endings I'd never known I possessed lit up like lightning, feeding my frenzy, my need. Seth's eyes roamed my body, his need and primal satisfaction at what he'd just done making me feel primal and seductive and beautiful all at the same time. He felt my pleasure at what he'd done just as much as I'd sensed his satisfaction.

"God, Dorian." His name was a soft plea, and he answered, lifting me from his lap and pressing me back down hard and fast.

"Turn her around," Seth ordered.

He didn't wait for Dorian to comply, simply lifted me from Dorian's lap and turned me so that I faced forward before lowering me over Dorian. By some kind of mutual understanding, he held me in place until Dorian placed his cock at the entrance of my pussy and lowered down. Fucked. I remembered the term was Reverse Cowgirl, but I doubted the woman had a plug in her ass or a second man in front of her. From behind, the plug in my ass was flat on the outside, but when it bumped Dorian's abdomen, his cock pushing deep, it was like they were both fucking me. Filling me.

My eyes were closed. My voice replaced by a primitive sound I didn't know I was capable of making. Dorian held my hips, pushing up off the bed, fucking me from below as Seth knelt before me. His mouth locked onto my nipples and his fingers found my clit, stroking me to orgasm after orgasm as Dorian pumped into me from behind.

Dorian's release pushed me over the edge yet again, his huge cock pulsing inside me, his emotions raging through me like a flash flood. I whimpered and let the tide take me, my body no longer my own.

The moment it was over, I was lifted from his arms, my back pressed to the soft mattress and Seth rising above me like an ancient god between my thighs.

"Look at me." It was a demand, no less.

I fought for breath and met his gaze. Waiting. I wanted him inside me. Fucking me. Making me his. I needed him just as badly as I'd needed Dorian.

When our gazes locked, Seth held steady, not letting me go, not letting me escape his claim as his hips rocked forward, filling me with his huge cock.

I lifted my hips to meet him, spread my thighs to take him deeper. He felt huge like this, the plug still in my ass, Dorian on his side beside us, watching. Making me hot. Making me feel beautiful.

"You're mine, Chloe," Seth murmured, shifting his hips to a fast cadence.

"Yes." There was nothing else to say as Seth pulled back and plunged deep. Hard.

He collapsed on top of me, his hands entwined with mine, pumping into me until we both exploded again.

When it was over, my mates lay on either side of me, each with a large hand pressed to my body. Covering me. Claiming me as Seth pulled a blanket over us all and we drifted to sleep.

hloe, Commander Karter's Office

IT WAS ODD STANDING IN A COMMANDER'S OFFICE IN NON-Coalition uniform. I was in a simple outfit of black pants and long-sleeved top. Comfortable, stretchy. Soft. No hard armor on them. No thigh holster. I felt more naked now than I was a short time ago when I was pressed between Seth and Dorian crying out their names with my pleasure. Again.

They'd practically kept me locked away in our quarters the last two days. Stripping me. Fucking me. Feeding me everything from chocolate to exotic alien fruits I'd never tasted before. Bathing me and doing it all again. I had never been so pampered in my entire life.

My pussy was a little sore—their cocks were impressive and it had been a while—and my nipples chafed against my utilitarian bra. I had a feeling they'd

73

held back a little since we'd only just met. I had no doubt that as time went on, they'd get wilder. More demanding. Less careful of their precious, fragile mate.

I couldn't wait.

God, had I been in the testing chair on Earth just two days ago? And now look at me. Staring down the massive Prillon commander of an entire battlegroup.

Well fucked.

Collared.

I felt the weight of it along the back of my neck, pressing onto my collarbones. It wasn't heavy, it was just...there. So were the ever-present feelings of Seth and Dorian. As soon as the collar went on, I felt connected to them in a way no one on Earth could ever explain. Psychically, perhaps. It was as if our brains were part of the same network. While I couldn't read their thoughts—which was a good thing based on the really pissed off looks on their faces—I sensed their anger, their frustration at being called to the commander's office.

Probably because they'd been completely and totally cock-blocked.

"You're the one who wanted me to hurry back to the ship to claim my mate, Commander. Seems a little ridiculous to pull us away from her after only a few hours," Seth said. While his tone was deferential, the words were anything but.

Commander Karter stood from his chair, came around his desk, leaned against it. "That was before I knew who your mate was. And why the hell are you here, Captain?" He asked Dorian.

"I'm Captain Mills' second, sir. We've claimed Chloe together."

"Yes, I can see that by the collars." Commander Karter looked to me. "You were matched by the testing program to one mate. Seth Mills. Yet in a very short time, you are here with two of my fighters. You accepted this arrangement?" His gaze landed squarely on the collar about my neck as he waved his finger between Seth and Dorian.

"Yes, sir," I replied. The testing dream had shown me two men and I'd liked it. Yet, I'd been matched to one. Or, had I always been matched to both Seth and Dorian without even them knowing it at the time? Had Seth's subconscious always considered Dorian to be his second? I had to assume yes since having those two fuck me had been even better than the dream. For once, reality outdid any fantasy I could imagine. I couldn't go back to only one guy after that. And Seth and Dorian? They'd ruined me for all other men. My pussy clenched in agreement.

Commander Karter nodded once.

Seth frowned. "May I speak freely, sir?"

"Haven't you already?"

Oh, I liked this guy. I could tell he was stern, but not an asshole. This ship seemed to be in the thick of battle with the Hive and he didn't have time to go hard-core by the rules. If he did that, nothing would get done. Bending and flexing, adjusting to the shit that hit the fan made a good leader. Unlike Bruvan. God, that was an asshole leader of epic proportions. He made decisions based on his ego, not the intelligence I provided. He was wrong. People died. Our ship got hit and I not only got injured, I was medical'd out and blamed for the whole disaster. Eight dead. A lost ship. Lost tech. And I got sent home while Bruvan got a new team and sympathetic pats on the back.

Typical bureaucratic bullshit.

No, Commander Karter seemed to have his shit together and could keep very alpha guys in their place. Although, he'd yet to push their possessive mate button yet. But it was coming. He knew who I was. As a Battlegroup Commander, he'd have full access to my file. I had a feeling I already knew what he wanted, and my overly protective mates weren't going to like it.

Seth shifted his stance, settled. Let out a deep breath. Dorian quietly loomed over us. Not the commander, for he, too, was Prillon and was enormous.

"We didn't expect to have to protect our mate from the commanding officer," Seth said. And there was the possessive mate I'd *just* been thinking about.

Commander Karter looked between the three of us, took in the black collars about our necks and the severe expressions on both of my mates' faces. He looked at me, his eyebrows raised in question. All I could to was shrug… and grin. If my new mates wanted to give me a little extra attention, I was game. To my shock, the huge Prillon commander threw his head back and laughed. "She doesn't need you to protect her."

Both of my mates bristled. Yup, protective. Possessive.

"What is that supposed to mean?" Seth asked.

Commander Karter lifted his hand. "Stand down, Mills."

Just two words and he expected two dominant, alpha males to chill out. I could feel the anger through the collars and the commander didn't seem to need a collar to sense it either. I wasn't sure where this was going, so I remained quiet. I learned long ago that sometimes it was best to just listen.

"Your mate isn't just a bride from Earth. She used to be a Coalition fighter. She's skilled enough to handle herself on the battleship." He cleared his throat and gave me a rather pointed look. "And elsewhere in space."

"We're aware she's a veteran," Seth said. "But we've... um, been a little too busy since she arrived to learn much about each other."

Was that a blush I saw creeping up Seth's neck? Adorable. Seriously. I wanted to go up on tippy toes and kiss him.

The commander cleared his throat, catching Seth's meaning.

"While she was holding your interest, her record held mine."

And here we go... Now I was the one blushing.

"I wasn't aware you paid personal attention to brides arriving on the battleship," Dorian added. He shifted to lean against the wall. While he looked relaxed, he wasn't. All he had to do was lift his arm and his hand would be back on my shoulder. With one quick tug of his left hand, I could be in his hold, with his right hand free to grab his ion pistol from his thigh.

"I don't. I let the Brides Program do their job. But when the doctor checked her out in the transport room when she first arrived, her profile pinged the ship's defense system. The doctor thought it prudent to bring her presence onboard my ship to my immediate attention."

Dorian reached out then, gently spinning me to face him. I had to tilt my head back...way back, to meet his pale gaze. "Why would your name ping the defense system?"

The darker tone he used with the commander was gone when he questioned me. He was softening his emotions for me; I could feel it through the collar as well.

I cleared my throat. "I'm sorry, Dorian, but I can't say."

So much for softened emotions. I felt a blast of frustration hit me and I stepped back. Dorian cupped my upper arm and held me in front of him, his touch amplifying the confusion and tension he, too, was feeling. And not in a good way. Wow, the collars were intense.

I rubbed at my neck. "Is there a way to turn these things down?"

"No." Seth was even more annoyed by my question, but he did a better job of calming his emotions so I didn't feel like I was in the middle of a volcanic blast of man-rage.

A V formed in Dorian's brow. "Why can't you tell us? Don't fear we'll judge you, Chloe. We're your mates. We are yours. Totally and completely. You can tell us anything."

"She can't tell you because she's not authorized to do so," the commander said from over my shoulder.

"If she can't tell us, then why the hell did you bring it up?" Dorian asked.

"Captains, I didn't request *your* presence in my office, I requested *Commander Phan's*. I have a mission brief for her. And a new assignment as a member of my command crew."

"What?" I asked, my interest instantly piqued. Yes! God. I'd been going crazy the last few months on Earth. The last couple of days with Dorian and Seth had been amazing. Hot. Sexy. Wonderful. But I couldn't have sex all day, every day.

Well, I *could,* but I needed more than that. Just like my mates did.

Doing nothing the last few months on Earth? Knowing the Hive was out here winning? Killing us. Destroying everything in their path. I couldn't sleep at night, staring up at the stars, knowing what was happening out here in space. I looked at the commander. "I am not allowed to return to active duty in my previous"—I searched for the right word—"capacity."

The Prillon commander nodded, not surprised. "I read your file. I am well aware of the—" He, too, looked up from his desk for a moment, searching for what he could say to me, without saying anything. "I have read your file. You will not be required to return to the field."

I slumped in relief. He knew about my past. My previous injuries. This weird thing in my head. And he was going to find a way to make it work to his advantage. And mine. I wanted to pump my fist in the air and whoop. But by the shocked dismay on my mates' faces, now was not the time. "I accept the position. Thank you, Commander Karter."

"Excellent, Commander Phan." He stood and walked around the desk, holding his arm out to me, warrior to warrior. "You'll be fourth in the chain of command for Battlegroup Karter. I'll expect you to report directly to me first shift tomorrow to meet the rest of the command crew and our operational team leaders."

"Commander Phan? Seriously?" Seth yelled like he'd just been struck by a whip. "You're a commander?"

Commander Karter crossed his arms. "Did you not

hear me address your mate as such? I can repeat it a third time if you wish. And outside of your private quarters, *Captains*, I suggest you address the commander with the proper respect due a superior officer."

"Is this a joke, Commander Karter? I am not amused." Dorian's tone was deceptively soft compared to the riot of emotions bombarding me through the collar.

"I was a commander," I said, holding out my hands by my sides to calm down my mates. Sheesh. Testosterone was great in bed, and not so great right now when their aggression and protective instincts were drowning me through our new connection. "I *was* a commander."

Commander Karter cleared his throat, speaking loudly. "Comms on. This is Commander Karter. Let the official record show that as of now, Commander Chloe Phan is officially reinstated as an active member of the Coalition Fleet, and as commanding officer overseeing the Hive ReCon and Communication protocols team." He was smiling at me the more my mates bristled. He was obviously enjoying this a bit too much. "You *are* a commander, Lady Phan."

"Lady Mills."

The commander waved his hand dismissively. "Not yet, she's not. That collar is still black, gentlemen."

Seth's voice was cold. Calm. "She can't be a bride and a Coalition fighter. We mated her, claimed her."

"I am well aware of the rules, Captain," the commander said. "However, that rule is in place specifically for active duty military personnel in combat positions. Serving me here, on the Karter, is not a forward combat position."

Seth strode across the room and stood beside Dorian so he could look at me too, study my face.

I put my hand to my neck. "Guys, you need to dial down the emotions. I sense you want to toss me over your shoulder and lock me in our quarters."

"The collars are working then, because that's exactly what I'm feeling," Seth countered. A little vein pulsed at his temple.

I looked at the commander. "I'll be on the command deck first thing tomorrow, sir."

"Excellent. You are dismissed."

I moved closer to the door and it slid open. My men stepped into the space, blocking me in. Their gazes roved over me, then over my head at the commander. Without a word, Dorian bent at the waist and tossed me over his shoulder. He spun on his heel and walked down the hallway. With his long strides, we were making fast progress back to our quarters. They hadn't said that was our destination, but they didn't need to.

"Be ready, mate," Seth said. "As soon as we're in private, you'll submit. And you'll tell us everything."

"I can't." It was the truth. Simple as that.

Dorian swatted my upturned ass once, then cupped it with his big palm. "I hate this, mate. I hate everything about this. But if that's the case, we're going to fuck you until you forget everything but our names."

Okay then.

hloe, Mated Coalition Fighter Quarters

"YOU ARE INSANE," I SAID, ONCE DORIAN PUT ME DOWN, and only so once the door to our quarters slid closed and Seth engaged the lock. That measure wasn't really necessary since I didn't plan on bolting, not that two huge mates would allow it.

"Perhaps, but discovering your mate is a *commander* with the I.C., you can't blame me," Dorian said working his armored shirt over his head.

"I wasn't keeping it from you intentionally," I replied, spinning on my heel and going over to the table in the small kitchen area and sliding my fingers over the smooth metal surface. I didn't want to look at either of my mates while we had this conversation. I could *feel* them, which was plenty.

"Strip, Commander," Seth said. He stood, legs shoulder width, arms crossed over his broad chest.

That made me look to him. Dorian took off his thigh holster, put it and his weapon on the table with a heavy thunk. His chest was so golden, the smattering of hair on it so fair. I remembered how silky it felt beneath my fingers, how warm his skin was, the play of hard muscle beneath.

I bristled, but since I felt the pulse of lust through the collar, my muscles immediately went lax and a little moan escaped my lips. He wasn't being demanding, like a Coalition fighter. He was being dominant as my mate behind a closed—no, locked—door.

And my mate wanted me to strip.

With fumbling fingers—not because I was nervous, but because their need coursing through my veins was distracting—I worked my shirt over my head as I toed off my boots.

When I looked up, Dorian was naked. All golden skin, brawny muscle and big cock. I licked my lips, eager for it. I knew what it felt like in my hand, how my fingers could barely close around it. I knew how it felt inside me, that flared crown stroking over every single sweet spot. I wanted it.

Dorian strode toward the bedroom and I stared at his perfect ass, the narrow hips and long, muscular thighs as he went. In the doorway, he turned, crooked a finger.

He didn't have to say a word. It was as if I were an Atlan bride and the collars were like mating cuffs, keeping us from being apart, even from the smallest of distances. Pulling me to him.

I took a step, but Seth's voice stopped me.

"Not yet, sweetheart. I told you to strip."

I was in my bra and pants and Seth had yet to move. He was watching me, liked how I was slowly revealed to him. It wasn't a strip tease. Far from it. The plain clothes and even plainer underwear were far from sexy. I told him this.

"I don't need to see you in lingerie to have you bring me to my knees," he replied. He put his hand over his cock, rubbed it and I could see the thick outline of it through his uniform. "This, sweetheart, is all yours. Just do as I say and you can have it."

His words were accompanied by a sexy grin.

All I had to do to have all of him was to get naked? Done.

I tugged and pushed, unlatched and dropped the rest of my clothes until I stood before him, the cool air furling my nipples.

Seth's gaze roved hotly over my body. He angled his head. "Good girl. Now go to Dorian. He's waiting for you."

I walked into the bedroom, felt Seth's eyes on me, heard his heavy footfall following.

Dorian was sitting on the side of the bed, knees splayed wide, cock curving long and thick so it touched his belly. I could see a glistening smear of pre-cum on the head and above his navel.

"Gorgeous," he said, his voice rough as he looked me over from head to toe.

I felt the word, knew the truth of it. They liked what they saw. Wanted me.

"You might be the one with the highest rank outside

these quarters, sweetheart, but here, with us, we run the show," Seth said from behind me.

I shivered, thinking of having the two of them dominate me. Oh, they'd taken the lead every other time we'd fucked, but they hadn't said it outright. I'd felt their control and let them have it. I'd *wanted* them to have it.

Now, was different.

"I didn't become a bride to work for the Coalition again."

Dorian looked up at me—a first that I was taller—and slowly shook his head. "A stupid way to go about it if you did. Volunteering, you're stuck with a mate, even if it's not the one you were matched to. There's no getting around it."

"And you're stuck with two," Seth added.

I spun about, put my hands on my hips. "You think I feel *stuck* with you?"

"Nope." Seth tucked a finger around his collar. "But there are more people impressed with you than just your mates."

Oh. I felt pride mixed with their frustration now.

"You're not mad?" I asked, biting my lip. I felt ridiculous standing around naked while talking about my military background, but it had to be said. It was an invisible, almost tangible...*thing* in the way.

"Fuck, yes."

"Not at you, mate," Dorian clarified. "Because we are your mates and should know everything there is about you. No secrets. Yet you have many."

"So do you," I countered. Being in ReCon, there was much they'd seen and couldn't mention.

"Exactly. And that's why we're frustrated. I was not

expecting a mate who had a past like ours. Experiences full of death, destruction. Evil. It is our role to shield you from that. And we can't. Now, with Karter wanting you back, it isn't just the past we want to ease."

I walked over to Dorian, stood between his parted thighs. His face was right in line with my breasts, but he wasn't looking at them. Instead, his pale eyes held mine.

"You're protective," I said.

He nodded.

"Possessive."

Seth stepped up behind me and I felt the coldness of the armor against my back. "Definitely," he replied. "That's our dried seed on your thighs."

Dorian cupped me between my thighs and I gasped. A finger slipped deep inside and I went up on my toes. "More here. Your pussy's filled with our seed. We've taken you enough that you could be pregnant. So when we hear you're wanted for dangerous Coalition missions? Yeah, we're angry. No way we'd let our mate—and baby—be put in danger."

He said all this as his finger slid in and out of me. He was right, their mingled seed made his movement easy. When he curled his finger, found that sweet spot that made me cry out, beg, whimper, I was at their mercy.

"I'm...I'm to ride a desk. Nothing dangerous." I could barely get the words out.

Seth leaned in, slid my hair to the side, his mouth skating along my neck. "You accepted the collars and the match before Karter's job offer. We're your priority. And we're going to remind you of that right now."

"Okay," I replied. What else could I say when just

Dorian's fingertip was enough to push me to the brink of orgasm?

"As I said, mate, we will make you forget everything but our names." I watched heat flare in Dorian's eyes as he said that.

"Yes," I replied, my eyelids drooping with the haze of need. I wanted just what they were offering. Shifting my hips, I began to ride that one digit, to fuck it.

A swat to my ass had me startling. The sharp sting of it having me cry out. To clench down on Dorian's finger.

To come.

I succumbed to the pleasure, the brightness of it, the sharp pain of the spanking. It all morphed and I felt the languid pleasure roll through me. My knees went weak and I placed a hand on Dorian's bare shoulder to steady me.

As soon as the feelings ebbed, another palm landed on my ass.

"Did we say you could come, sweetheart?"

Seth. Perhaps it was the fact that he didn't have ingrained customs as Dorian and the Prillons that he was the one who was the Dominant. That's what he was, his true colors. He wanted to master me, not only because he got off on it, but because I did, too. He *knew* it made me hot.

Hell, one quick spanking and it pushed me over the edge. I'd barely been spanked before, so I had no idea it was a kink I liked. But with Seth? I pushed my ass back, at least as far as I could since I was still riding Dorian's finger.

He slid from me and stuck it in his mouth, sucked and licked it clean.

Seth's hand came down but on the other butt cheek. I gasped, feeling my breasts sway from the impact. "You like that, don't you, sweetheart? You don't have to say it, we know because of the collars. We can feel how your body heated, your pussy got wet. Hell, you came because of a little hint of pain."

Dorian grinned as he studied my face. "Bend over, mate, and suck my cock."

Seth laughed as I knew he could feel the wave of desire that coursed through all three of us at Dorian's words. Without realizing it, I licked my lips.

I did as Dorian said, placing my hands high on his thighs and leaning down. His cock was right there, ready for me. I swirled my tongue over the tip like a lollipop, licking up all his pre-cum.

"I taste you on my tongue and with that hot mouth of yours, I'm not going to last."

Dorian's words had me smiling around the thick crown. Power swelled through me, at least until Seth spanked my upturned ass again, and I took the cock deep into my throat.

"Fuck," Dorian groaned. I felt his bolt of pleasure as I swallowed and tightened around him.

Retreating, I took a breath. Seth moved away. I couldn't see him from my position, so I focused on Dorian's cock. If I could get him to come, it would show that I could still be in charge. That I had the power.

"Topping from the bottom," Seth said, coming back into the room. "I sense it. You want to get Dorian off to prove something, not to make him feel good."

Was I?

I pulled back, took him from my mouth completely as

I looked up at him. He tangled his fingers in my hair, held me in place.

"I just wanted you to come," I admitted.

"Because?" he asked, pushing.

"Because I could make you."

He gave a soft smile, pulled me up by the back of my head so he could kiss me. I tasted myself on his tongue, our flavors mingling. Salty, musky. Potent.

When he pulled back, his pale eyes held mine, our lips only an inch apart. "We're taking control, mate. Not because we're stronger, but because you'll give it to us. A gift. And when you suck my cock, that mouth will be offered for my pleasure. And yours in the service of the act."

"Submission," I said, the word sliding off my tongue as my arousal slid down my thigh. Yes, I wanted them to be in control. I wanted him to fuck my mouth instead of the other way around.

"We'll take your worries, your burdens. Everything. All you have to do is obey. Submit," Seth said.

"Feel," Dorian added.

"Yes," I repeated, wanting that with a longing that made my pussy ache. My clit throb.

"Yes, sir," he clarified. "Or yes, mate. Nothing else."

His deep voice settled me into my role as much as being between them. I had a commander with professional aspirations for me. A weighty role I hadn't asked for but was forced into. I wanted it. Oh, I wanted to be needed again. It felt heady to be so desired.

But that was as a fighter. An I.C. specialist.

Not as me. My name could have been interchanged

with anyone else on my team and Karter would have been equally thrilled to have him or her on board.

But Seth and Dorian wanted me. Me! Only *me*.

I'd been matched to them. I was theirs. So submitting to them wasn't a choice I thought of. It just was. Subconscious. Deep within me. I didn't need to control Dorian by an incredible blow job. He'd come, sure. But if I offered my mouth to him, my laving tongue, my throat, he'd still come, but I'd be gifting him, just as he said, with my service of the act.

Outside these quarters, I was Commander Phan. Here, now, naked and exposed, vulnerable, I was Chloe Phan, mate. They wanted only what I could give them. No one else. They wanted the most precious gift of all, the one that was the most difficult to give but the most precious to receive. My will.

"Yes, sir," I said, meeting Dorian's gaze, giving him a quick nod. I looked over my shoulder at Seth. "Yes, mate."

I felt the thrill, the heat, the need circle between us through the collar just before a resounding sense of authority drift over me.

Not mine.

Theirs.

I didn't have to worry about working in the Coalition again. I didn't have to worry about what was in my file. Or Bruvan. Or being knowledgeable as a codebreaker, the lives that were at stake if I made a mistake. The baby they wanted to make with me. I didn't have to worry about anything but what Dorian and Seth said next.

"Suck me, mate."

I lowered my head again to Dorian's cock. This time,

with a gracious heart, an open spirit and a need to bring him pleasure.

"Yes, mate. Just like that. Good girl."

I felt Seth's hand slide over my pussy lips, wet and slick proving I was ready for them. I gasped at the gentle feel, which only made Dorian groan.

He had no interest in my pussy, only used my juices to coat my ass, so that when his hand settled on the small of my back and his thumb rested between my parted cheeks and settled right there, he could circle it and press in without discomfort.

I didn't have to think about what he was doing. I just had to feel. So I wrapped a hand around the base of Dorian's cock—my fingers didn't even touch in my grip—and slid it up and down as I took as much of him as I could.

A cool dribble of lube slid over my back entrance and was worked in by Seth's thumb, circling and pressing intently until the broad digit slipped inside. From the angle, it was almost hooked within me, but settled easily.

When Dorian put a hand on my shoulder and lifted me off his cock, I was surprised. At myself because I'd focused solely on the hot length of him in my mouth, the flared crown as it nudged my throat, of breathing, of the way Dorian breathed. I'd been so focused on him. Intent.

"I want my cum in your pussy, mate. While I know you'd swallow it so well, we won't get you bred otherwise."

"Yes, mate," I said, remembering his words.

His thumb came up, swiped over my damp lip. I could only imagine how I looked, lips probably red and swollen, my eyes glazed with need. No doubt he could see Seth's thumb disappear in my ass as he looked down my back.

Seth dropped to his knees, but didn't move his thumb from me; it was still just inside me, stretching me, keeping me open.

Dorian hooked a hand about my waist, slowly pulled me toward him. "Climb on, mate."

Seth moved with me so as I settled over Dorian's cock, took him deep, his palm still rested on my lower back, his thumb sliding deeper into me.

"Oh god," I said, my eyes falling closed. This double penetration was intense. Dorian's cock was so big, so thick he was practically splitting me in two. But with Seth's thumb? I was so filled.

I felt Dorian's sharp spike of desire as I clenched and squeezed around him, Seth's satisfaction at my taking them both so well, at submitting.

"Ride Dorian's cock, Chloe. Up and down, take it so deep he'll spurt all that cum up into your womb."

Seth was an expert at dirty talk. I'd never imagined a guy's cum being hot before, but now they were claiming me with it, marking me, *breeding* me as Dorian had said. I should hate it, but I didn't. Nope, it was going to make me come. Having them come in me, their seed filling me, finding that egg that would take it in and make a baby, made me so fucking hot.

"Yes," Dorian groaned. I hadn't realized I'd said the last out loud because he added. "We'll keep you full of cock and cum, mate, until we give you that baby."

Seth worked his thumb into me, deeper and deeper until I could feel it end, then he worked it out, how he was going to ultimately fuck me with his cock.

"I can feel your need to come. Don't."

I whimpered. "Seth, please."

"No. You'll wait for Dorian."

Dorian's hands came to my hips, his grip tight as he began to move me as he wanted, to lift and lower me in a quick pace.

Sweat dotted his brow, his teeth gritted together. I felt him thicken in me as his breath came out in harsh growls. "Now," he commanded.

Seth pulled his thumb all the way out, then slid it back in. The sharp bite of that stretching pushed me over the edge and I came with Dorian, my scream filled the air as his fingers dug into my hips, his growl rough against my neck. "Yes, your pussy's milking all that cum from me."

I felt his cock pulse, the heat of his cum deep inside me. It was wild and rough. Dark and dirty. Carnal and primitive. I loved it.

I could barely catch my breath as Seth pulled his thumb from me once and for all. Dorian's hips continued to pump up into me, then slow. Still.

When he lifted me off his lap, I felt his seed slip from me, down my thighs. Seth spun me about, pulled me down so I straddled his thighs. I felt the roughness of his pants against my sensitive skin, felt the brush of his cock against my belly. I didn't remember him opening his pants, tugging his cock out, but that's all he'd uncovered. Besides the ruddy colored cock aiming straight for me, he was fully clothed.

"My turn."

He lifted me up, settled his cock at my entrance, then pushed me down onto him so I was filled in one long, deep stroke. I was so wet with Dorian's cum it didn't hurt, but the stretch made me gasp. The deepness of him made me pant.

With a hand on my hip, Seth rolled us so I was on the floor on my back and he loomed over me. His cock was deep and he began to move as he watched my face. The abrasive feel of his armor against my nipples had me arching my back.

"More?" he asked.

"More."

He thrust.

"Deeper?"

"Deeper."

He thrust hard.

Dorian dropped to the floor at my side, took hold of my knee, opened it wide and back so it was practically by my ear, spreading me for Seth. Making me take him deeper. Just what I needed.

Pride and desire, excruciating pleasure and possessiveness swirled between us until there was no me. No Seth or Dorian. Just us.

And when Seth came inside me, filling me to overflowing, they weren't done.

No. They had much to prove, for while I was a commander, I was their mate. Under their complete control.

And all night long, I did as they wished, because they were right. When I submitted, I soared.

8

S *eth*

As I escorted my mate down the hall to her first day at her new post on Commander Karter's control deck, I worried, but I also felt a unique sense of pride.

Chloe was dressed in civilian officer's clothes, the pale cream color making her skin and hair look even more vibrant. She wore no makeup—not that many females on the ship did—and didn't need any. Her black lashes framed her green eyes to perfection. As we walked, I couldn't tear my gaze from her curves, the ones I'd touched and kissed the night before. I couldn't stop thinking about what we'd done, how she'd submitted to us. And now, I couldn't stop staring at the command bars on her collar and chest. My mate was a fucking commander. She outranked almost everyone in this entire battlegroup except Commander Karter himself and a handful of others. And yet she'd been on her knees before both of her mates, relinquishing the control she wore about her like her uniform.

I'd had her naked and pliant. Calm and submissive beneath me. Yet now, outside our quarters, she could give me orders, send me into the fray just like every other commander on this ship. And for some reason, that made my cock stir.

"Too bad you're not still holding that plug in your ass," I whispered, leaning down as we walked so only Chloe heard me.

She stopped in her tracks, tilted her chin up to look at me. Oh yeah, that was a commander's narrowed gaze. "You're in charge in private, Captain. Out here, I have as much chance of having a plug up my ass as you do."

I got hard just listening to her tough talk. We'd kept her filled with cock and plug until it was time for her to get ready for her job. I wouldn't have minded her having that reminder lodged deep inside her that, a reminder that she belonged to Dorian and me while she worked, but she was right. That wasn't going to happen.

She patted my chest, went up on her tiptoes and whispered directly in my ear. "Don't worry. My pussy's achy and a little sore. I won't forget who I belong to."

I cleared my throat, stepped back when two Everians walked by. They saluted Chloe and continued on, completely unaware of our topic of conversation.

"Good," I said. There wasn't anything else I could say standing in the damned hallway without dragging her into the nearest maintenance room and fucking her again. So I took her elbow and continued on down the corridor.

I wasn't sure what Chloe had done in the past for the

Intelligence Core and I no longer wanted to know. Knowing would just drive me crazy. It wouldn't be anything good. Or safe. Her job wasn't working with small children in a pre-school. She didn't grow plants in the nursery. Nothing protected and sheltered like that. No, whatever she'd done had been dangerous as fuck, and I'd probably get an ulcer just thinking about something in the past I had no control over.

We were about to round the corner, and I knew this would be my last moment of privacy with her for a while. I had no doubt I'd be called up for another ReCon mission sometime soon. I didn't really have time to waste, but I couldn't leave without tasting her, without leaving her with more than just the aftereffects of a long night of fucking. Passing Everians or anyone else were just going to have to deal. She was my mate and I would give us both what we needed before we parted.

I stopped dead in my tracks and backed her against the wall, claiming her mouth for my own. To my relief, she lifted her arms and wrapped them around my neck, burying her fingers in my hair. Yes, she was as desperate as me. She molded herself to me the way I'd come to expect and had only ever dreamed about before she was in my life. Her kiss was as hungry and eager as mine.

"If you get called out while I'm working, be safe. You better come back to me, Seth," she murmured against my lips.

"I will." Our gazes locked and held. I couldn't give her empty promises and we both knew that war didn't wait for love. And we were at war. Yet, I said it anyway because I meant it. If I got pinged for another mission, I would deal with the fucking Hive and do whatever I had to do to get back to her.

Lifting my hand, I used my thumb to trace her bottom lip before planting one more quick kiss on her lips. "Behave in there."

She laughed, the devil dancing in her eyes. "You know I can't promise you that."

I buried my hand in her hair at the base of her neck, tugged it back so she could do nothing but look at me. Through the collars, I felt her arousal at the slight nip of pain at the rough hold. I didn't say a word, didn't need to remind her of my dominance. Only then did she practically melt in my hold, submitting so beautifully that every protective instinct I possessed came roaring to the fore. I pulled her close for one more, hard kiss. "I love you, Chloe. I know it's probably too soon to tell you, but I wanted you to know in case—"

She lifted her fingertip to my lips and stopped me. "Don't even say it. And I love you, too." I knew the truth of it even before she spoke the words. Felt it from my collar, to my heart, to every cell of my body. Hearing her say them settled something in my chest, something hard and resolute, something unforgiving, something absolutely determined I return to her. This wasn't over. Far from it. The Hive weren't going to rob me of her.

Our fingers entwined as I walked her to the command deck. The door slid open and Commander Karter was there, his arms crossed, a scowl on his face. I could tell by the look in his eyes he was relieved to see her...and that worried me.

"Welcome to the command deck, Commander Phan." Commander Karter raised his arms and ordered everyone to be silent. "Officers, this is Commander Phan, formerly of the Intelligence Core. She's ours now, and although she's no longer technically a military commander, she has years of experience in the battlefield. She's come to us as an Interstellar Bride and I have given her the rank of Civilian Commander. You will follow her orders and give her all due respect." He turned back to us and held out his hand, indicating a chair in front of a complex communications array. "Commander, your station."

She squeezed my fingers tightly and I pulled her into my arms once more, uncaring who watched, and whispered in her ear, "I love you, Commander. Stay out of trouble."

"I love you, too. Now get the hell out of here so I can do my job, Captain." Her smile made me grin and I nodded with respect to Commander Karter before stepping back.

Chloe was fire and sass and I loved everything about her.

The door slid closed, locking her away from me and I turned back toward our private quarters. I needed to shower and prep for the day, be ready if I got pinged. I'd rather stay and wait for Chloe, but I'd be nothing more than a parent dropping a child off for the first day of kindergarten. I was whipped. Completely. I admitted it. At least to myself. Dorian was, too, but he wasn't here for us to commiserate. We were probably the only two male fighters in love with a commander.

I grinned even as I picked up the pace. Chloe wasn't the only one with a job to do.

———

Dorian

I WAS AWAKENED BY SETH STIRRING IN THE ROOM. I HEARD a boot hit the floor, then the other. He stuck his head in the door to the bedroom.

"Where's Chloe?" I asked, finally awake enough to realize I was alone in bed.

"I just walked her to the control deck. You sleep like the dead," he replied.

"Chloe wore me out." I couldn't help the grin that spread across my face or the way my cock swelled. "Why don't you get some more sleep?"

He raised a brow, shook his head slowly. "I'll share a bed with you, but only if Chloe's between us."

"I can't believe she's our bride and she's off on her first day of work as Commander Phan," Seth replied. "Not Lady Mills." The words were tinged with bitterness.

I climbed from the bed, grabbed my clothes off the floor, worked them on. "We can't be angry with her for being smart and successful in her career."

I was quite proud of her, actually. But that didn't mean I wanted her going out into battle any more than Seth did. Good thing she couldn't. For once, I was thrilled with the rules and order of the Coalition.

"I hate that we can't know her past. It's like there's this fucking gap of four years about her we'll never know." He unstrapped his thigh holster, set his ion pistol on the table.

Someone was a cranky bastard this morning. Considering we'd fucked our mate into exhaustion last night, Seth should have been a whole hell of a lot happier than he was. He didn't look or act well fucked. He was behaving like a child whose favorite toy was taken from him.

"Fuck, this hard-on isn't going down. I kissed her in the hallway and, shit, I'm ready to have her again." He sighed. "I can't go to a briefing like this. My superior would have my hide. I'd never hear the end of it."

I could relate. My cock was wide awake this morning and ready for another round with our mate. We'd worked her hard, but she'd loved every minute of it. We'd dominated her all night long. I said as much to Seth. "I bet she's squirming in her desk chair."

"I took the plug out before we left."

The thought of her with an ATB plug in her ass, stretching and preparing her for our claiming, had precum drip down my cock head. "Still, I'd be surprised if she's walking right."

That got a grin out of Seth. "She said she's achy."

I groaned. She wasn't the only one. My balls were going to ache all damned day until I could sink into her again.

"I have to go shower and take care of my dick before I can go anywhere." He tugged his shirt over his head, let it fall to the floor as he strode out of the room. I heard the bathing tube kick on. He was out of sorts. I couldn't blame him. We had a mate, a mate who wasn't between us in bed, all meek and tame. No, Seth had to be matched to a feisty, submissive commander of the fucking Coalition.

She was perfect for him, for us. The fact that she was strong-willed, independent and full of sass just made us both want her more, made her surrender in the bedroom that much sweeter.

So we'd check on her, but let her do her job. Then when she finished, we'd strip her bare at the door, leave her role as commander there, too, and clear her head of everything but us.

"Get moving," I shouted into the other room. "I want to see our mate. I don't give a shit what Karter thinks."

Seth stuck his head out of the bathing room. "No fucking way. Trust me. We're totally pussy whipped. I've admitted it and you need to as well. We can't just go barging into the control deck looking like Chloe has us tied by a string to our balls."

Shit, he was right.

"Fine," I replied, not thrilled. I picked up my pillow, dropped it back on the bed to get it just the way I liked it, then rolled over onto my belly. Shit, my cock was not going to let me lay that way so I turned on my side. "I'm going back to sleep. I'm sure I'll get called out soon enough."

9

hloe

I'D BEEN SITTING AT MY NEW POST FOR SEVERAL HOURS scanning for high frequencies, listening for anomalies. Four years of training came back to me slowly, bit by bit. I could still do the job, the experimental NPU in my skull assured that. But without the adaptive headpiece unit, I was at a disadvantage. Since there wasn't one on the Karter, and he hadn't mentioned it, I had to assume no one here was aware of the technology. It wasn't my place, or rank, to share something that was top secret.

No matter, I'd make this work.

I was excited to be back at a post, feeling like a member of the team. I'd never been good sitting idle, and I was more than relieved to discover that I would have a place on this battleship doing a job that mattered. Helping to fight the Hive.

At the same time, I could satisfy my mates. Not just sexually, which was pretty darn amazing, but emotionally as well. I knew how much they didn't want me going on a mission. I felt it through the collars, saw the way they'd behaved with Commander Karter the day before. Heard them say the words. I'd compromise, meet this need in them to keep me safe. And in return, they'd give me what I needed. A safe place to relinquish all control, to be protected and cherished as I did so. I could just be me. Chloe Phan, or Lady Mills. Not Commander. They'd mated me, not the high-ranking officer.

The constant hum and buzz of activity on the command deck was comforting. I'd missed it. Missed the consistent routine of a well-oiled machine, of officers who knew one another so well they could anticipate each other's moves in the eye of the storm.

Commander Karter stood like a statue of marble in the center of the room. Nothing seemed to faze him. But I recognized the mantle of command that settled on his shoulders as he let his teams do their jobs. He was what the crew needed him to be and so I would be, too.

I returned my attention to the communications panel. The provided headset I wore was so ancient, I had removed it in frustration for the third time when I looked up to see Commander Karter standing before me holding a small box that I recognized. I gasped. Not so top secret after all. "How did you get that?"

"I don't know what you're talking about, Commander Phan," he replied, his voice deep.

"But isn't that what I think it is?"

Commander Karter placed the small box in front of me carefully, delicately, as if he knew exactly how valuable the tech inside was. He left the box and lifted his hands away. "I don't see anything at all, Commander. I'm quite sure that Dr. Helion, of the Intelligence Core, wouldn't see anything either." He lifted a brow and grinned, one eye moving oddly, in the closest thing to a wink I had ever seen from a Prillon warrior.

I grinned back and opened the box with shaking hands to find my old I.C. headset, the most advanced of technology. Even among the fleet. So rare that no one outside my division at I.C. had ever seen one, at least not that I knew of. But Commander Karter seemed to be rewriting all kinds of rules, just for me. He cleared his throat. "I trust this will make your job easier."

I could only nod as I slipped the odd earpiece over my head and waited for the metallic click and familiar hum in my head as it connected with the NPU implanted in my skull, just beneath the skin. I felt like a walking computer when I wore it.

The device amplified sub-human frequencies and slowed down encrypted codes and Hive communications to give me time to hear them. It was as if I had turned on the radio and could hear a familiar and comforting song. "Yes, sir "

He nodded and seemed pleased with himself. Although, it was no wonder why. My division in the I.C. only had about a dozen codebreakers like me. And it was a very big war, spanning hundreds of star systems and Coalition worlds. "Only you are allowed to touch it, Chloe. It will be kept in my safe when you are off duty. You will give it to me or to the officer on deck at the end of every shift so that one of us can lock it up."

"Yes, sir."

"That device doesn't exist, and it doesn't leave this room. Meaning, your mates can't know."

I bristled at his words, having him think I would ever betray a job-related secret. But I remembered he'd never had one of his commanders mated to fighters before. I was the oddity and the connection I shared with Seth and Dorian was close. Perhaps too close, especially with the collars. He was wise to offer the warning, but it was unnecessary.

"I understand, sir." And I did. This was dangerous technology. I was shocked they'd allowed Commander Karter to get his hands on it.

But then, not every battlegroup had an ex-I.C. officer who knew how to use it. Like me. And not every Coalition sector was locked in daily battle with the Hive, like Karter's battlegroup. Sector 437 was notorious for being a living hell, the one place most sane warriors dreaded to go. The only warriors happy to be here were glory hounds or trigger-happy adrenaline junkies.

Ironic that for me, it was the opposite. I was happier than I'd ever been in my life, and it had nothing to do with the war, and everything to do with my mates.

I sat down and started my work again from the beginning, this time deciphering exponentially more of what I heard. The complex computer software that the Coalition Fleet used for standard operations could decode most Hive transmissions on their standard frequencies, ship to ship, or across space. But the internal connections of their Hive minds were more intuitive and less machine-like than one would guess. There was a rhythm and flow to them. Something I instinctively understood, something their computer systems had not yet been able to crack because it was too organic. Not illogical. Too human.

I sat back in the chair and continued to work for several hours, comfortable knowing my mates were occupied. It felt odd to be in space again, yet with mates. I was surprised how often my mind turned to them. Dorian, I knew, was sleeping. After they'd fucked me into exhaustion, I'd heard a ping calling him to a late flight mission. I didn't know how long he'd been gone, but when he climbed back in bed, he'd kissed me, wrapped his arms around me and promptly fallen asleep.

And now, while I worked, Seth was heading out with ReCon 3 on a mission. I monitored his activity, could hear the reports from the communication station across the room. I would know instantly if anything happened to ReCon 3 or Seth. I realized I would be spending a lot of time in this room, waiting for news when one of my mates was out on a mission.

How I had fallen in love with both of them in just a few days? I couldn't begin to explain, even to myself, but I had.

I craved their touch. I craved Seth's intensity and Dorian's protective embrace and not because I felt it— them—through the collars. I raised my fingers to mine. I had become addicted to their strength, their dominant alpha male attitudes and to the way they touched me when we were alone. The way they made me feel. I had never known anything like it. And I knew instinctively that I never would again.

They were mine, just as I was theirs.

A strange humming in my head pulled me from my wayward thoughts and I focused all of my attention on the task at hand, scanning for high frequencies and trying to decipher any communications I might come across.

But this wasn't *stumbling* upon anything. This was like a cannon blast in my head and I doubled over in pain. Crying out, I bent over on top of the control panel, everything spinning and cutting into my mind like a tornado of sharpened blades slicing through my skull.

Every eye on the room turned to me in surprise, but I could not lift my head. The pain was building, not receding, like a dagger had been shoved through my ear drum into the center of my skull.

"Commander Phan?"

I tried to lift my head, tried to sit up straight, reached for the NPU attachment on the side of my head and covered it with my hand before Commander Karter could take it from me. "No. Don't touch me. "

The commander stood before me, hands on his hips, no hint of amusement in his face. "Talk to me."

I tried, but the problem was, I had no idea what was going on. It was as if I had suddenly stumbled into a Hive communication hub. So loud and so filled with traffic that it was like standing in the middle of a rock concert. Except I couldn't plug my ears. And I was standing right in front of the speakers. "It's loud."

"Commander Karter, medical needs you."

Commander Karter turned and nodded "Put it on screen."

A Prillon warrior I did not recognize filled the display. His green uniform the only indication of his rank. Behind him, a human woman, a doctor in a dark green uniform and Atlan mating cuffs, was trying to calm an Atlan that I had never seen before.

The doctor on screen wiped his brow. Panting as if he had run a marathon and was out of breath. "The Hive is doing something, Commander. Warlord Anghar sat bolt upright from a ReGen pod, screaming and clutching his head. And he'd been unconscious."

I wedged myself up onto my elbow for a better view of the Atlan. The pain inside was like a knife in my skull, but no longer a surprise. I could endure.

Commander Karter studied the doctor and the Atlan and I wondered if he worried the warrior would turn beast. "How much Hive tech is still inside the warlord?"

"I've taken out everything I can," the doctor said wearily. "He'll have to live with the rest..."

"Is he himself? Am I looking at Warlord Anghar, or am I looking at a Hive Drone?"

The doctor shook his head and ran his hand through his auburn hair. "I don't know, sir. He's been unconscious in the ReGen pod for two days until now. He popped up and scared the hell out of all of us. No one has spoken to him yet."

"Can he hear me?"

The doctor nodded. "I'll put you on, sir." He turned away from the screen. "Warlord Anghar, the commander would like to speak with you."

The Atlan lifted his eyes to the screen and it seemed that everyone on the command deck was holding their breath, waiting to see what we would be dealing with. A sane man? Or a beast that could rip the entire ship apart. His hands were fists at his sides. "I hear you, Karter." His voice was a deep rumble, but sounded sane.

Commander Karter leaned forward, as if he could get closer to the Atlan. "Excellent. Be on the command deck in five minutes." He turned to me, narrowed his gaze. "I want you in my office, now."

He walked into the officers' meeting room. I rose to follow, but dizziness swamped me and I had to stop for a moment. Palms on the control panel, I regained my balance as the Prillon warrior next to me stood and held out his hands to assist. But I waved him away.

"I'm fine, thank you..." I took three deep breaths and ignored the pain. I walked into the meeting room and took a seat next to the commander. We waited in silence at the large oval table until the doctor and the beast known as Angh entered the room. The Atlan barely cleared the doorway, he was so big.

The commander indicated that the warlord should sit at the opposite end of the table. Before I knew it, the room filled with other warriors I did not know, but whose command insignia made it clear that they were the commanding officers for each section of the battlegroup crew.

Conversation flowed around me as the doctor gave the warriors in the room an update on the warlord's condition. He was remarkably quiet for an Atlan. Well, any alpha warrior, really. It only went to prove to me how much the warlord had been through, or how much pain he might be in. The doctor mentioned that a large number of Hive implants had been removed, but a few remained and could not be taken without endangering his life. He would be transported to The Colony as soon as arrangements could be made and transport codes approved by Prillon Prime. The Atlan warlord was clearly not happy about it, his hands in tight fists on top of the table. But like all warriors banished to The Colony, there wasn't a damn thing he could do about it and we all knew it.

I, too, had a variation of Hive technology implanted in my body, but it was Coalition controlled, specially modified by the Intelligence Core, and, at the moment, driving me completely insane. Luckily, despite the constant buzzing, the pain had faded to a dull headache. Yay, me.

The commander must have said something to the doctor when I wasn't looking, for he walked over to me and placed an injector to my neck. Within moments, the pain was gone. I breathed a sigh of relief. "Thank you, Doctor."

The doctor nodded and sat in the empty seat next to me. The dark circles under his eyes and the lines around his mouth indicated that he was utterly and completely exhausted by his forty-eight-hour ordeal with the beast.

Commander Karter looked to the warlord at the end of the table.

"Thank you for attending, Warlord. Since you are well enough to be out of the ReGen pod, what do you know about what's going on?"

I didn't know what was going on and was eager to find out. I was a little confused, as if I'd missed something big. But, it was my first day on the job, so I definitely had some ramping up to do.

The Atlan blinked slowly, watching everyone in the room as if seeing them for the first time. His eyes weren't totally silver, like some I'd seen on those who'd been integrated, but they shimmered from the inside. The poor man was looking through eyes that were no longer his own.

And I thought the weird buzzing in my head was an adjustment.

"It's a trap, sir," he said, his voice deep.

10

THE ATLAN CLEARED HIS THROAT, THE SOUND A THICK rumble in the room. "They're using this Sector to deploy a new, experimental weapon..." The warlord's hands were palm down, flat on the table, but his entire body strummed with tension so thick I could feel it on the other side of the room. "You have to get the entire battlegroup out of here."

"You know I can't do that," Commander Karter replied. "The Coalition has held Sector 437 for hundreds of years. We're not going to lose it today." When Angh didn't say more, the commander sighed, then asked, "What kind of trap?"

The giant Atlan shook his head, frustration on his face and in his crumpled brow. "I don't know, sir. I don't remember everything. I know there's a trap here. I know it's closing in on us. But that's all I've got."

"Well, Warlord Anghar, I guess that's better than nothing." Commander Karter turned to me. "Tell me some good news, Chloe. Tell me you can hear what these bastards are planning. Give me something to work with."

All eyes in the room turned to me, most with curiosity. I was new here and the commander was placing the entire mess in my lap, looking for answers. I lifted my chin. "There's nothing obvious in the normal traffic. I'll need a couple of hours to analyze their signals and see what I can come up with."

"What was that attack about? The pain in your head."

"Not sure," I replied. I wasn't. I had no idea why it suddenly came on other than I'd intercepted…something.

Angh's hands balled into fists but he did not lift them from the table. "You don't have two hours. I can feel them getting closer."

So could I. I had no idea how, but I just knew.

I looked into Warlord Angh's eyes and an understanding passed between us. Somehow, he knew that I could feel it, too. There was a strange humming connection between us, as if the frequencies that the Hive used to transmit were tying us together. Two fixed points on the end of a vibrating guitar string.

I looked away from the giant warlord to Commander Karter. "He's right. We don't have two hours. I can feel them, too."

"With all due respect to Commander Karter, what the hell are they talking about?" I didn't recognize the Atlan warlord who spoke, but he was massive and scarred and wore the rank of commander on his uniform.

The Atlans voted for their leaders. So, the warrior before me had been elected and chosen by the others. Respected. Experienced. He saw me watching him, his eyes jumping briefly to the Prillon collar around my neck before he bowed slightly at the waist.

"My Lady, I am Warlord Wulf."

"Commander Chloe Phan, of Earth."

The giant warlord towered above me in my chair. He was nearly eight feet tall.

"And what is your specialty, Commander Phan? How did you earn the rank of commander in the coalition fleet?"

Commander Karter stood and leaned over the table, his elbows locked, arms straight and tight, his muscles bulging with barely restrained tension as he rested his knuckles on the table. "Commander Phan was with the Intelligence Core for four years. That is all I can tell you. But we need her help on this. What she says, goes."

One of the other officers shifted around at the far end of the table. I could not see his face clearly, but I heard his words. "Shouldn't we alert the Intelligence Core of this new threat?"

"Gods be damned, yes." Commander Karter stood to his full height and rolled his head on his neck. The ominous sound of bones cracking was loud in the room. "Send an immediate transmission to the I.C. We need a team here, now."

He looked down at me. "Commander Phan. Get on the communications array and get me anything you can about this."

I didn't know what *this* was, but I only said, "Yes, sir." I stood, inclined my chin to the warlords and warriors in the room, but especially to the commander and Warlord Anghar before returning to my station.

I sat once again and lifted the specialized headphones to my ears. They formed nearly half of an old-school football helmet on my head. It was bulky, and ugly. Heavy. But I had a pop-up display screen that showed communication patterns and in the peripheral vision of both eyes. More importantly, the rest of the noise from the command deck faded to nothing. I was working in a bubble, my own silent, still bubble.

But it wasn't quiet. The opposite, in fact. My senses were constantly bombarded with space noise that crashed through my headphones like ocean waves pounding the surf.

And I had to listen for the one small murmur of something alive. Something more machine than man.

It started off as a faint ping to my senses. As quiet as a kitten's whisker pressed to a window. Barely there, but I heard it, and I zeroed in on the sound like a bloodhound. Like a great white shark who had just sensed that single drop of blood in an ocean of water.

My mate was out there. Seth was out there with ReCon 3 right now. Dorian would leave on another flight mission soon. If the Hive was setting a trap for all of us, I would find it. Those merciless machines weren't going to take my mates from me. They weren't going to destroy anyone in this battlegroup. Not if I could help it.

The old familiar rage welled up in me, but with it came a laser-like focus I hadn't felt in over a year. This was combat. This was the kind of war I knew. The type of battle I won.

I homed in on the signal, eliminated other traffic

noise, amplified the sound until I had just that nearly silent signal floating in my mind like a repeating drum. Over and over. I pulled the pattern of sound up on my display screen shocked to discover that it created a honeycomb-like structure. The sound bounced from one nexus point to the another in a series of entwined hexagons.

It looked like a net and the entire battle group was headed right for it.

I jolted to my feet, yelling, "Commander Karter, stop the ship! All ships, full stop."

In two steps Commander Karter was at my side. "What have you got?"

"It's a trap, just like the warlord said. I don't know what's out there. But it's some kind of net, or a network, and we're about to run into it."

The commander took one look at my screen and didn't ask for more details. He raised his voice, giving the command to bring every ship in the battlegroup to a full stop at once. I didn't know how close we were, exactly, to whatever was out there, but we were close. God only knew what would happen if we ran into it. Or if the Hive were waiting on the other side.

The ship shuddered beneath my feet, jerking to a stop with such sudden force that I knew anyone who had been in bed sleeping, had most likely just rolled out and hit the floor with an uncomfortable thunk. But that was the least of our concerns. Another officer raised his head. "Commander, incoming, Transport 2. It's the I.C. Do you want me to clear them for transport?"

"Yes. I'm on my way." He turned and pointed at me. "You're with me."

I nodded with a shudder. I was afraid that I knew exactly who was transporting onboard this ship, and I had absolutely no desire to see him ever again. In fact, it was probably a good idea to stand behind the commander, so I didn't kill Bruvan the moment I saw him.

We were almost out the door when one of the officers raised the alarm. "Commander, Freighter 572 is not responding to the stop order. We've got no response."

The commander turned on his heel and walked over to the officer's station where he viewed a three-dimensional readout of the battlegroup that hovered above the flat display area. The entire group of ships had come to a stop at his command, hovering in the air like little holographic models. All except for one ship.

The commander turned and looked over his shoulder. "How many warriors do we have on that ship?"

The officer he spoke to looked down. "Two, sir. Two Prillon warriors. Entry level pilots who just arrived from Prillon Prime a few weeks ago, sir. They are probably sleeping."

Commander Karter stood. "How far ahead of the battlegroup are they?"

"Two thousand miles and gaining."

"Keep trying to contact them." He turned to look at another officer. This one was so close to human looking, I knew he had to be from Trion. "If you can't reach them in the next two minutes, take control of their ship remotely and turn it around."

"Yes, sir."

I had just turned back to the door when an alarm sounded. The commander spun once more. "Report."

The officer who had been trying to contact the

freighter before frantically pressed buttons and moved his hands through the air as if he could conjure the holographic image from empty space. The small shape that had been bright red, the little blip in the air that represented the freighter, was gone. "We just lost the freighter, sir."

"What do you mean, we just lost the freighter?" Commander Karter walked over to the holographic image, his boots silent on the hard floor, that silence a measure of his tightly reined control.

The officer didn't look up from his station, but continued with his work as he spoke to the commander. "The ship disappeared, sir. It's gone."

The commander turned to stone in the cold room. "I want a visual. I want it now."

As quietly as I could, I walked up to stand behind him, unsure of what I would see on the screen, but knowing it would be horrible. The entire command deck was silent as we watched the single freighter sailing through what seemed like the deep blackness of space before suddenly exploding in a violent flash of light.

"Again," the commander ordered. The footage replayed three more times as we all watched and tried to analyze what we were seeing. No obvious shots fired. The explosion started on the outside, the hull of the ship, not from within. Yet there were no enemy ships in the vicinity, no Hive, no missiles or ion blasts or cannon shots. Nothing.

One minute the ship was fine. The next it exploded.

The Transport Officer cleared his throat. "Sir, the I.C. just arrived in Transport 2."

"How many?"

"Eight, sir."

The commander was still looking at the screen, at the drifting fragments of the burning remains of the ship and the two pilots who had been on board. "Call the ReCon teams back. Get our assault teams back here. Abandon Latiri 7. We need all available troops back here to protect the battlegroup. And make sure they have coordinates to avoid that net."

"That'll take hours, sir." The XO, a giant Prillon warrior named Bard approached. "If we give up the ground we've gained on Latiri 7, the Hive will double their forces on Latiri 4. It'll take us months to get it back."

Commander Karter lifted his hands to the Prillon's shoulder. "I know. But we all know we're not in Sector 437 to win the war. We are here to maintain the status quo, to prevent the Hive from advancing into Coalition space. This is where we drew our line in the sand, Bard. If we can't hold them back, if the entire battlegroup is attacked by a weapon I can't see, we'll lose this entire sector."

The Prillon wasn't happy, but he wasn't going to argue. He knew the commander was right. We'd all just witnessed the instant destruction firsthand. We all knew what was at stake. Half a dozen Coalition planets would be within striking distance of the Hive if the Battlegroup Karter fell. "Get everyone we can back here. We hold Latiri 4. They can occupy themselves on 7 for a few days while we figure this out. I want every ship in defensive formations around the battlegroup. I want every shuttle and civilian transport pulled in tight, battle formation."

"Are you expecting an attack, sir?" the Prillon asked.

"Warlord Anghar said the Hive laid a trap for us. I'm

afraid we've just triggered it."

"Yes, sir."

The commander walked out as Bard started giving orders for all ReCon teams, all assault teams, all freighters and all pilots to return to battle group. With an emergency code I had only heard of, but never witnessed in use.

The commander walked down the hallway not bothering to check on me until we were within a couple of minutes of Transport 2. When he stopped suddenly, I almost ran into his back.

As he turned to face me, the cool-headed commander was gone. And in his place stood a very angry Prillon warrior who had just lost two pilots and was not happy about it. "What am I dealing with, Chloe? Who's going to be in this room?"

I shook my head. "I don't know, exactly. Probably an I.C. communications team, or a Hive infiltration unit. If that's the case, they'll have someone like me."

"Someone like you." His gaze wandered up the side of my face to the odd silver attachment that I still wore over my ear. The odd metal formed to my skull, creating a working circuit, a connection between it and the NPU below my ear. "Someone wearing one of those things. Someone who can hear them?"

After I nodded, he grabbed my shoulder, as he'd done to Bard, and squeezed gently, so I'd know he had my back. "Good. We need all the help we can get. I'm not losing another ship." He turned and walked into the transport room.

I was on his heels and held back a groan at the sight that waited for us. There, standing on the transport pad, chest puffed out like a pompous ass, was my old teammate, Commander Bruvan. And, exactly as I had predicted, he had a fully armored Hive infiltration unit behind him. The unit was made up of special operatives recruited by the Intelligence Core to get into places and get out without the Hive detecting our presence. Like SEALs on Earth, but with better technology.

A Hive Infiltration Unit was a highly specialized branch within the Intelligence Core. An active unit usually consisted of one codebreaker, like me, a communications operative with a specialized NPU implant programmed with additional Hive communications protocols. We were the eyes and the ears, the Coalition's most specialized weapon against our enemy. We were the only ones who could hear them.

Not everyone who was outfitted with the experimental NPU could decipher their odd language. Most of the time, it was gut instinct, not hard data, that came through the system—which left a lot of room for error. Mine. Bruvan's. When we guessed wrong, people died.

The rest of the team was made up of highly trained weapons specialists and two demolitions experts who knew exactly where to strike in a Hive controlled area, inside a Hive operated vessel or station, and bring the entire thing down as efficiently as possible.

And their commander?

Our eyes met and I felt the familiar fury rise within me. It was Commander Bruvan, and he looked about as happy to see me as I was to see him. I ignored the hulking Prillon warrior to inspect the rest of his crew.

Thankfully, he did the same, stepping forward when

Commander Karter greeted him. "Welcome to Battleship Karter. I am Commander Karter."

Commander Bruvan held out his hand and they clasped arms like warriors. "I am Commander Bruvan, and this is my team."

Commander Karter inspected them quickly, but thoroughly, and I knew he missed nothing, not the specialized sniper rifles, not the Hive tech implanted in their armor or the heavily packed demolition bags loaded with explosives. Commander Bruvan looked up. "How long ago did you detect the Hive transmissions? I need to speak to the officer who detected them. A Warlord Anghar?"

Commander Karter nodded his head, but did not move other than to turn slightly and lift his arm in my direction. "Actually, Commander Phan detected the signals we're dealing with. Warlord Anghar warned us of a Hive trap. But she's the one who found it."

Commander Bruvan looked at me and I looked at him. I felt like I was in an Old West showdown.

"Bruvan."

"Phan." He crossed the distance and stood before me. Toe to toe. I would have said nose to nose, except he was at least a foot taller. And towered over me, as I'm sure he intended.

I put my hands on my hips but didn't step back. I looked up to find him scowling at me. "Show me what you've got, Phan. And then stay the hell out of my way."

Oh yeah, I'd volunteered to be an Interstellar Bride, to ensure I was as far away from this one particular person in the entire universe. Yeah, that hadn't worked out so well.

11

THE BATTLE ALARM SOUNDED, JOLTING ME INSTANTLY ALERT from a dead sleep. I threw on my uniform quickly. I remembered Chloe was at the control deck, safe with Commander Karter. Seth, I knew, was out on a ReCon mission. I'd heard his comm unit ping when he was in the shower earlier and had quickly dressed and run out before I fell back asleep.

I grabbed my weapon, holstered it.

Seth faced the same uncertainty we all did every day, and we'd both come to terms with it. I just hoped Chloe could, too.

Uniform and boots on, I left our private quarters and made it to the pilots' debriefing room in record time where I was shocked to find Chloe standing with Commander Karter and Warlord Anghar on the edge of the room. A few feet away was a group of warriors I did not recognize. Their armor was strange, embedded with odd silver circuitry that I recognized well as Hive tech.

Their leader appeared to be glaring at my mate and I did not like the way he looked at her. Hell, I could tell just by looking at him he was an asshole. But I could sense that from Chloe through the collar, knew she was more than familiar with this man. She hated him. But he underestimated my Chloe's fire, for she glared back, not backing down one inch. I felt shame tinge her pride, her resolve to stand her ground.

My pride at having such a brave, beautiful mate swelled even as the seriousness of the situation slammed home. Every pilot we had was in the room. No one was sleeping. Commander Karter himself walked to the front of the group and began briefing us on our mission which, for now, was a basic scramble alert. We had to be ready to go at a moment's notice. Apparently the giant Atlan we'd taken off that freighter with ReCon 3 had woken from the ReGen Pod and warned the commander of some sort of trap. That my Chloe was in the middle of it didn't surprise me at all. But I could feel a shocking mix of emotions coming from her. Emotions I had no hope of deciphering now.

Shame. Guilt. Fear. Rage. Resolve.

There was no softness in her now. She was a warrior.

It felt like she was already engaged in battle.

I'd be going out soon and I breathed a sigh of relief when the commander informed us that all ReCon and assault teams had been called back to the Karter as a precaution.

"Pilots, head to the flight deck," Commander Karter said. "Be prepared to depart at my command. Good luck."

I was leaving then, but Seth was on his way back. He would be here. Life or death didn't matter to me any more or less than it ever had. I wanted to live, but I had to fight. The only thing I cared about as we were dismissed was making sure my mate was protected.

I rose and made my way over to Chloe, who was surrounded by Atlans and Prillons who seemed twice her size.

I pulled her aside and drew her into my arms briefly, just so I could take her scent, her touch with me into battle. I wrapped my arms around her and she squeezed me tightly. I placed a soft, lingering kiss on her lips. I felt her need for me through the collars and I was sure she felt the same in return.

"Come back to me, Captain," she whispered. "I'm totally in love with you."

My heart threatened to burst at the words. The feeling coursed through me, and I couldn't hold back what I felt for her. She sensed it through the collars, but I wanted her to hear it, too. To know the truth of it all. "I love you too, mate, to death and beyond."

I let her go, but walking away from her was one of the hardest things I had ever done. I knew she'd be safe on the battleship right next to Commander Karter, but Seth wasn't here. Not yet. Both of us would be out there, in danger. But it was the best I could do.

 *orian*

"WHAT ARE WE DOING HERE, IF WE'RE NOT FLYING THE freighter? It's our ship." The Prillon pilot seated next to me in the freighter's launch bay looked as unhappy as I felt. His name was Izak, and we'd been flying together for two years. He was a damn good pilot, perhaps even better than me. But he wanted answers I didn't have.

"I don't know. But we've got the I.C. on board, so the gods only know what kind of bullshit we're about to get tangled up in."

Izak groaned and leaned forward, elbows on his knees and his head in his hands. "Can you hear that?"

I stilled and listened, really listened. Nothing. "No."

"They gave me this damn armor, and now I can hear them." He rubbed his temples before sitting up and leaning his head back against the wall.

"Who's they? Who gave it to you?"

"The I.C."

Intelligence Core. "And you hear them? Who can you hear?"

His eyes met mine. "The Hive, Dorian. It's the fucking Hive."

The Hive. The I.C. Strange armor and stealth ships? Yes. We were fucked.

We were in a small launch bay, where we'd been told to report. Two stealth shuttles sat at the ready. They wouldn't hold more than a handful of crew, less than ten warriors, and that was if everyone onboard was standing in the tiny cargo area directly behind the pilots. The ships were designed to be infiltration units, used to do collect intelligence behind enemy lines, and I had a very bad feeling about where this mission was going.

"What are they saying?" I asked. Izak's armor was different than mine. I wore the standard issue black camouflage for space ops, but his was filled with silver streaks and odd circuitry that was unmistakably Hive.

He shook his head. "Can't understand a damn thing. It's like buzzing insects inside my head." Izak started taking his armor apart, dropping pieces on the floor. "I can't fly like this. By the gods, I can't."

Izak stripped in record time, then walked, naked, to a flight cabinet and pulled out new armor. He was bending over to put on the pants when the mission doors opened and in walked a dozen people, including Commander Karter and my mate. Chloe was dressed in the same silver streaked armor that Izak had worn and my heart plummeted into my stomach.

No. Gods, no. She was supposed to be sitting at a desk,

not wearing battle armor. And was that an ion cannon strapped to her thigh?

The beast, Warlord Anghar, was behind her, wearing similar tech. The only one not wearing battle armor was Commander Karter. He called for Izak and I to join them, and I remembered the warrior's naked state. A hot flame of jealousy rose up as I thought Chloe might see the warrior's body. But when I looked up at her, she was staring at me, only me, with so much love in her eyes my throat threatened to close up. Her emotions flooded me through the collar. Love. Hope. Fear. Resignation that we were all going on this mission, and that we might not come back.

Gods, no. I didn't like that coming from her. Not at all.

I grabbed Izak's chest armor, threw it at him and nudged him on the shoulder. "Come on. Hurry up. Karter is here."

Izak followed me, putting on the rest of his gear as we walked across the deck. When we reached them, it was obvious that there were two very separate groups. The Intelligence Core had a full infiltration unit of eight wearing the special armor that Izak had just removed. Then there was Chloe, Anghar and two Prillon warriors serving as guards or protectors, I wasn't sure which. The commander rattled off everyone's names and I noted the way Bruvan glared at my mate. He also wore the strange silver attachment over his ear that Chloe did. Hers was the first I'd seen, but I recognized Hive tech when I saw it, and seeing that thing attached to my mate's head like a parasite did not alleviate my fear for her.

Short introductions over, the commander cleared his throat. "All right, warriors. You all know why you're here.

We need to get that net down. We're sitting in the middle of a trap and I don't like it. But we also need to know how it works and how to detect it. They could be deploying this weapon in other sectors, targeting more battlegroups. We need to know what we're dealing with and how to destroy it."

Karter turned to me and Izak. "Captain Kanakar, you will be piloting the shuttle with Commander Phan and Warlord Anghar. Your team is to operate in a support position. Coordinates and instructions have been loaded into the shuttle's system. You will take your orders in the field from Commander Phan. Are we clear?"

"Yes, sir." I nodded. The commander made a point to force me to acknowledge that Chloe was to be the commanding officer on my shuttle, but I didn't mind. I was too flooded with relief that Chloe was in the support team and wouldn't be part of those going out there, into space, battling the gods only knew what kind of Hive treachery.

"Captain Morzan," he addressed Izak. "You will be piloting the assault shuttle. You will take your orders from Commander Bruvan."

"Yes, sir."

Commander Karter looked at us, hard. "I'm not going to insult you two by reminding you of your rank and the rules of command, but this isn't a standard op. This is I.C. Do you understand?" He stared directly at me when he said the last, a second blatant reminder that Chloe would be giving the orders, that my mate outranked me, and that even if I disagreed with her decisions, it was my duty to follow her authority. No matter the danger.

Fuck.

We both nodded, but chills raced over my skin and a feeling of foreboding weighed down my limbs. Izak seemed unaffected, but he wasn't heading into a war zone with his mate to protect.

If she'd let me protect her.

Commander Bruvan spoke, "I am ranking officer on this mission, followed by Commander Phan. Once we leave the ship, we will operate on short wave radio frequencies only. No exceptions."

"But we'll be out of range for communications with the Battleship Karter," Izak said.

"Exactly." Commander Bruvan lifted his helmet onto his head. "Load up. Let's do this."

Izak and I exchanged a warriors' goodbye, holding each other by the forearm, and we each led the way onto our small shuttles. In a matter of minutes my mate, the warlord and the two Prillon warriors were behind me and I closed the shuttle doors. Chloe sat in the co-pilot seat and, to my shock, helped with the launch sequence. "What other secrets do you have for me, Commander Phan?"

"You'll have to wait and see, Captain." She smiled at me, her face framed by the black helmet she wore, and my heart felt light, despite the fact that I was probably heading out to the most dangerous mission of my entire career with the Coalition Fleet. With her beside me.

As fast as it appeared, her smile was gone, and a commander was seated where my mate had been moments ago. Chloe was all business, her focus and determination clear through the connection we shared in our collars. "Follow the other shuttle. We're going to drift in close to the net and do some scans before we decide how to disable it."

Warlord Anghar stood directly behind us, and the two Prillon warriors behind him. There was standing room only on the tiny ship for warriors so big, and no privacy.

I concentrated on flying, on what I knew, and followed Izak's shuttle out of the launch bay and away from the battlegroup. I saw nothing ahead of us, but I knew we'd lost a freighter. Something was out there.

"I can hear them." The deep rumble of Anghar's voice washed away the last of my contentment at having Chloe beside me. The warmth and love flowing between our collars ended abruptly, replaced by cold dread. Her next words replaced any lingering warmth in my body with a chill.

"So can I. And they know we're coming."

———

Chloe

The net was massive. Much larger than anything I'd ever seen before and I realized that in my job with the Intelligence Core, we'd only ever seen test cases of this weapon, small deployments done by the Hive to test its effectiveness.

This was something completely different. It was huge. Thousands of miles across and nearly invisible to sensors. A battlegroup moving at high speeds would be completely destroyed before they realized what had hit them.

Shocking Dorian with my piloting skills was the one bright spot in this mess. All I.C. officers were required to have basic training in piloting a vessel, just in case they happened to be the last man standing, the only option for an escape. I'd only ever flown once before, and that incident had forever cemented Bruvan as an enemy, and gotten me kicked out of the Core. But it had saved my life. And his.

Ungrateful ass.

Whatever. I couldn't focus on the past, not with a massive network of Hive explosives forming a net around Battlegroup Karter and the two men I'd grown to love. One of whom sat beside me now, so much devotion and protective mojo flowing through our collars that I felt damn near invincible. The feeling was heady and addictive, and increased my determination to survive this mess, to make sure that this time, nothing went wrong.

At drift speeds, it took us nearly an hour to reach the perimeter of the network of Hive mines. Behind me, Warlord Anghar knelt on one knee, his hand on the back of my chair, massive head scanning ahead of us as if he could see them with his eyes.

He couldn't. None of us could. They were invisible to the naked eye. And to most of our sensors.

But not to me. Or Angh, through our special technology. And we were close.

"Stop here," I ordered Dorian and we stopped moving as Bruvan's shuttle drifted closer to the network.

"I don't see anything," Dorian said.

"Trust me, Prillon, it's there." Angh's face moved side to side, his gaze roaming the huge monitor in front of us. "Can you magnify the screen, Captain?"

"Of course." Dorian's hands moved deftly and the images before us magnified, far off stars growing in size until they filled the screen with fist sized beacons of light.

"Enough." Angh shook his head and waved a hand. "They are very well hidden."

I agreed. It was disconcerting, how strongly I felt the presence of the Hive weapon, yet could see nothing. It made me feel like we were chasing ghosts.

But that freighter blowing up wasn't from a ghost. Those men died because something very real was out here.

"What now, Commander?" Dorian turned to me and I shook my head.

"Turn on your low frequency radio. We wait for Commander Bruvan's orders."

"For how long?" Angh asked.

I wanted to snort with disgust, but kept it professional. Barely. "Knowing him, at least an hour."

Dorian didn't say a word, but his annoyance came to me clearly through the collars. As, I was sure, my dislike of Bruvan was shared with him.

Sure enough, an hour passed with no word from Bruvan or his crew on the second shuttle. Angh paced the tiny confines of the rear of the shuttle, the two Prillon warriors pressed with their backs to the wall to give the agitated beast as much room as possible. Even with their accommodation, he could only take three steps before turning to repeat the process.

I was used to this, to Bruvan's head games. He claimed he took so long to make his decisions because he needed to analyze all the data first. But he and I knew the truth. The real analysis went on inside our minds, where the special NPUs we both had implanted in our skulls worked overtime breaking down Hive communication and codes.

I was support only. Both Commander Karter and

Commander Bruvan had made that absolutely clear. So I hadn't butted my nose in Bruvan's business. But something wasn't right. I was sure Bruvan could feel it, too. That was probably why he hesitated now. And Angh's pacing? I had a hunch that Atlan beast could hear a lot more than he wanted to.

"Do you hear it, Angh? The deep hum in the background? Behind the buzzing of the others?"

"Yes."

I stood, walking toward him. "What do you think it is?" I wanted his take on it, in case I was mistaken, or making things up in my head.

"It's their mother."

"Yes!" I jumped up and hugged him briefly. As he stood, stunned, I rushed back to the copilot seat and pulled up the communication with the other shuttle.

"Commander Bruvan, this is Commander Phan. Do you copy?"

"This is Captain Morzan. Commander Bruvan is not onboard, Commander."

"What?" I felt my jaw go slack. "What do you mean, he's not onboard? And why wasn't I told?"

"Orders, sir." The Prillon warrior was unapologetic.

"Can you patch me through to him?"

"Yes, Commander." Izak paused a moment and I could hear him moving in his bulky armor. He was a big Prillon warrior, with a very nice... I cut that thought off before I could finish it. "Commander Bruvan. Do you read?"

"This is Bruvan. Go ahead, Captain." Bruvan's voice was distant, coming from his helmet audio. I knew where he and his team were—floating in space with jet pods strapped to their backs.

"Commander, this is Commander Phan. Where are you?"

"We are approaching a nexus point of the grid."

"Why wasn't I told? What is the plan?" I was fuming, anger welling inside me like a volcano. How dare he endanger all of us, his crew and mine, simply because he didn't like me? Let us sit here and stew for an hour while he suits up and goes on a space walk with his entire team? Asshole.

"It's need to know."

"As your support team, I believe we need to know, sir." The sir came out closer to a snarl, but I didn't care.

He sighed, audibly, as if I were the most annoying human being in this sector of space. "Very well, Commander. We are approaching the nearest nexus point along the grid. Once there, my demolition team will place explosives and destroy it, creating a chain reaction that should bring down the entire net."

I cleared my throat and Angh's snarl let me know he was thinking the exact same thing. "That won't work, sir. One of our freighters hit the net a few hours ago. It destroyed the ship, but the net remained in place."

Commander Bruvan's reply was short. "We are using a very special type of explosive, Phan. Designed for this type of situation."

My head began moving side to side before he even stopped talking. "Sir, there is an object floating behind the net controlling them all. If you listen closely, you will hear an almost imperceptible rumble. Warlord Anghar and I believe it is coming from some kind of master control mechanism."

Angh spoke to Bruvan. "It's their mother. It controls all of them."

Commander Bruvan was silent for a full two minutes, and I held my breath as he was most likely listening with the same experimental NPU that I had. Surely, he would hear it. He had to. There were too many lives at risk for a mistake.

"I hear nothing, Commander Phan. And Warlord Anghar, all due respect, you are too heavily contaminated with Hive technology to give a trustworthy opinion."

Angh growled, but I held out my hand to keep him back from the pilot area. "Bruvan, please listen to me. Commander Karter wanted Warlord Anghar on this mission for a reason. He wanted us all here for a reason. We have to work together, not fight one another and not get caught up in the past. Please. I am telling you, blowing up one mine isn't going to do any good. We have to take out the mother."

Beside me, Dorian had my back. "Taking out any more of their mines could trigger a full-scale Hive assault, Commanders. One hit could be attributed to flying debris, a meteor or asteroid. Space junk. But two might tip the scales, alert them to the battlegroup's presence here."

"Duly noted, Captain. Commander. But I am in charge of this mission and we are going to destroy this thing. Now."

"Yes, sir," I muttered, slumping back in my seat as Dorian, Angh, the two Prillon warriors and I sat quietly and listened to their microphone chatter. The two explosive experts placed their mines and the team reconnected, drifting as one back toward their shuttle.

Once safely inside, they would detonate the explosive and we'd all run like hell.

"Back us off, Dorian. I don't want to be anywhere near that thing when it blows."

"Yes, Commander." My mate's voice was all business, but the collar let me know the truth. He was relieved to be taking me farther away from danger. We drifted back, Dorian using the ship's thrusters to push us gently away from the net without triggering any possible detection systems.

But we weren't out of the proverbial woods yet, not even close.

Bruvan and his team made it to their shuttle, and he gave Izak orders to get them back to a safe distance.

They had just broken away from the net as we watched when the first ion blast hit the other shuttle in its right rear engine. Above us, like a giant wall of awakening monsters, the network of mines appeared out of nowhere, abandoning their cloaking to attack the small ship. The network of mines didn't explode, but fired massive ion cannons the size of our freighters.

"Holy shit," I whispered.

"Get out of there, Izak!" Dorian yelled, but it was too late. A second blast hit their left engine shell. Then a third struck their hull.

The main communication line opened and Commander Karter's voice roared through the speaker in my helmet. "Get back here. Now. We're under attack from the rear. A full armada of Hive vessels. All ships return to defend the fleet."

"By the gods, they've got us cornered." Dorian turned

in the pilot's chair to look at me. "We're trapped. The entire battlegroup is trapped."

"Seth's out there somewhere," I said aloud, more to myself than anyone else. Of course, he was out there. Everyone in the battlegroup was out there. And would die.

Angh leaned forward, over my shoulder, watching as Izak's shuttle spun out of control away from the net, back toward the fleet. "An armada. We'll never survive that many ships. They'll completely destroy us all."

"No, they won't." I knew it with a certainty that made my teeth ache with cold. "They don't want to destroy us." The Hive had no intention of destroying anything. They wanted Drones. More Soldiers. More organic material to integrate into their system. They were like cannibals, and they never got full.

"No!" Angh's roar was deafening in the small space, and I stood, looking at him, waiting for him to calm down. I knew what we had to do. I could *feel* it in my bones.

"You done, warlord?"

Dorian's head snapped to me, suspicion and anger fighting a war within him. I had no doubt he was confused by my calm, the certainty I felt. But if anyone on this ship understood what I needed to do, it would be the beast in front of me. He could hear them, too.

All four warriors turned their complete attention on me but I didn't panic. It was like an out-of-body experience. I felt...nothing.

"Warlord Anghar and I are going to put on external armor and slip through that net to the other side. The mines are placed at intervals. He and I can hear their communication links, so they should be easy to avoid." I looked up at Angh, who listened intently, his huge eyes blinking slowly as he registered what I was saying. "Once we are on the other side, we'll track down the master control node and approach it using the jet pods."

"Destroy their mother," said Angh. He was already reaching for the special armor attachments that would allow us to go outside the shuttle, into the cold blackness of empty space.

"We'll load up with explosives, track the motherboard controlling the entire net, and blow it up. Once the net goes down, Commander Karter can escape the Hive attack with the rest of the battlegroup."

"You don't know where this mother control pod is," said one of the Prillon warriors. I hadn't learned his named, or his friend's. "If you wander too far on the other side of the net, or fail to take it down, we won't be able to reach you."

The other Prillon looked at Angh, then held my gaze. "If you are trapped on the other side, the fuel pods will not be enough to get you back to the ship."

Every word they said was true, but this had to be done. We couldn't lose the entire battlegroup. All those people. Five thousand of them. And not just warriors, but kids. I looked up at the beast. "That a problem for you, Angh?"

He held my gaze. We both knew what was at stake. "No, my lady. It is not."

I turned to Dorian before he could explode with the emotions I felt building inside him. "No one else can do this, Dorian. We're the only ones who can hear it. It's going to be invisible, shielded, just like the others were. If we don't find it and destroy it, the entire battlegroup will be taken. Integrated. Even the children. This entire sector will fall. We protect six planets, Dorian. Billions of lives. We have to try."

Dorian didn't argue, simply pulled me into his arms and squeezed. "You better come back to me, mate."

"I will." I had to. It was possible I already carried a child, and that child would *not* be born into the Hive. Integrated from birth. The baby's fragile mind and body destroyed.

I'd rather die.

The Prillon warriors stepped back and to the side so Angh and I could reach the special armor we needed to propel ourselves through space.

We suited up as fast as we could, the warriors each checking and double checking our suits for us as we slipped into them for this battle.

Dorian handed Angh a bag full of explosives.

"I need one, too. Just in case."

Behind me, a Prillon warrior handed me a similar bag. I groaned as I lifted the straps over my shoulders. It had to weigh at least sixty pounds. But once we were drifting in space, weight would mean nothing.

"Ready?" Dorian shouted from the pilot's seat.

"Ready," I shouted back. Angh and I stepped back into the small decompression area at the rear of the ship. We had to stand close, the space was small. The big warlord's hand reached for a heavy line about six feet long and pulled it from the wall to hook us together at the waist. We might drift, but we'd do it together.

The door slid into place, separating us from the rest of the shuttle. I reached up and placed my palm flat on the glass in front of us. Dorian lifted his hand to mine on the other side of the panel.

"I love you, Dorian."

The words were the last I said before the rear of the craft opened and Angh and I were ejected into deep space.

13

"ReCon 3, come in. This is the Karter."

I leaned over my pilot's shoulder as he pressed the communication switch. "ReCon 3. Mills here."

"Captain, this is the Karter. We are under attack. The battlegroup is trapped between the net and a Hive armada. Your orders are to rescue the I.C. team from shuttle 547 and return to the Karter immediately for battle orders."

"Fuck me." Trinity stood to my right. Jack behind her.

"An armada? How many Hive ships is that?" Jack asked.

"Too fucking many. Get that I.C. team back here. Karter out."

The line went dead and the shock of our situation

Seth

moved through my team like a ripple over a still pond. These were battle-hardened troops. Experienced, both on Earth and out here in space. We'd never even heard of a Hive attack of this scale.

"Well, let's go rescue the spooks and get our asses back to the Karter, people." I leaned down and patted my pilot on the shoulder. "What do we have on the scanners?"

"Two stealth class shuttles. 546 has lost both engines and is drifting."

"Lost both engines? How the hell did that happen?" I peered at the screen and identified the small ship. Sure enough, the back end of the shuttle looked like it had been the main course at a charcoal bar-b-que.

"That looks like ion cannon fire," Trinity said.

"Yeah, but from where?" Jack asked.

There was nothing in front of us but empty space, but we'd all heard, in our briefing before takeoff about the invisible net, about the freighter that blew up. So I knew something was out there. I'd never felt like space had a personality or presence of its own. It always felt empty to me. Like...nothing. But now, staring out into the darkness, I would swear I felt something more. Menace.

"Get some grappling hooks onto that shuttle and let's pull her in. I've got a bad feeling about this." I lifted my head and tilted my chin to the side so my whole team would hear. "Helmets on, people. Full lock. We could lose pressure at any time."

I pulled my helmet on my head and made sure the locks were airtight, the hissing sound of the helmet seal reassuring as something caught my attention floating across the screen. I pointed. "What is that?"

The pilot messed with his controls, but the co-pilot

answered. "That's shuttle 539. Stealth model, sir. Her engines are operating at full capacity."

Chills raced over my flesh as we got closer until suddenly, Dorian's emotions flooded me, nearly bringing me to my knees. Dorian was on this ship. And he was holding on by a thread. Something was very, very wrong. "Hail that shuttle. Now."

The pilot did so, and sure enough, Dorian's voice answered the call. I didn't bother with formalities. The emotions bombarding me told me too much already.

"Where is she, Dorian? What's wrong?"

Dorian quickly recapped the mission, the argument between our mate and Commander Bruvan, Bruvan's decision to blow up one of the hubs of the net, and the fact that my mate was, at this very moment, strapped to an Atlan and floating in space on the other side of that net with no way back but the fuel canisters strapped to her back.

"Fuck. Fuck. Fuck. How could you let her go?" I asked, but I already knew the answer. He'd had no choice. Neither of us did. She was a commander. A warrior. We either loved her the way she was, or we walked away.

And *that* was *not* happening.

"Forget that, Dorian. I know you had no choice."

Dorian's chuckle was reassuring, but held no mirth. "You're right about that. Just like you have to go save Izak and everyone else on that shuttle and leave Chloe to me."

I wanted to leave Bruvan to rot, but that wasn't an option either. And Izak was a damn fine pilot. A good warrior. I had to go. "Damn it. I want constant reports, Dorian."

He understood. I knew he did, because the concern for

our mate flooded both of us at the moment. And immediately after that emotional tidal wave passed, both of us hardened our resolve. Duty. We would do what we had to. For Chloe. For everyone. We were soldiers and we had a job to do.

"You know what I know, Seth. After you connect to the other shuttle, you might want to keep your ReCon team close for a couple extra minutes. In case we have to go after her."

"Copy that." The pilot closed the comm and I turned to my team. "Let's go save the asshole who put my mate's life in danger."

Trinity grinned at me. "You thinking it's time for another demotion, Captain?" She referred to the last time I'd had a problem with another ReCon captain's orders. That jerk from Earth had cost me two men and wrecked my ship, all because he refused to break off pursuit of a Hive Scout vessel. And *that* after we'd just saved his ass from an Integration team. He'd been hours away from being one of the Hive himself.

I understood his rage at the time. But when he took command of my ship and got us all into a battle we couldn't win? Well, my fist found his nose when we made it back alive. After that punch, I'd been a lieutenant for about three months. But his nose was still crooked and he couldn't look me in the eye.

Totally worth it.

"Absolutely." I grinned back.

———

CHLOE

SPACE WAS COLD. THAT WAS MY MAIN THOUGHT AS ANGH and I drifted closer and closer to the buzzing network of explosives trapping our people for the Hive attack. Not just cold, bone numbing, silent cold. Like you were lost. Nowhere. Utterly and completely alone.

Even as the thought crossed my mind, Dorian's resolve flooded me through the collar and I knew I wasn't really alone and never would be again. I had my mates now. They were connected to me. They were mine. And if I ever wanted to see them again, feel their touch, kiss them...well, I had to live. Which meant I had to stop the freak-out and focus on what I was doing.

Angh tugged on the line connecting us until we faced each other and he wrapped his arms around me. "We have to be small."

"I understand." I wrapped my arms around his waist, or as much of it as I could, and held on. It wasn't intimate in the traditional sense, not with enough armor and explosives between us to blow up a small moon, but it was intimate in another way.

We could both hear the mother calling, the nexus of the net, that thing which was connected to the Hive mind. We were, in a way, one with the Hive. And in that, we understood each other, too.

"We're close to the net. Don't move," Angh instructed as he used his fuel pods to navigate us through the space between two Hive mines. It hummed around us as we drifted by, crackling with energy like the sparks of static I used to get when I forgot fabric softener and had to pull my fuzzy sweaters out of the dryer.

Except I knew it wasn't static cling, and if it zapped us, we'd be dead.

The gap between Hive mines was almost like floating through a short tunnel. Soon, we emerged on the other side, the hum of the net much quieter, but the pull of the master control hub loud. Too loud. It was everywhere. And nowhere.

Angh released me when we were clear and we drifted, side by side, both of us scanning the area, looking for our target.

"I don't see anything. Do you?" I asked.

"No, but I can feel it."

"Me too." Our communication seemed to be disabled on this side of the net. I could no longer hear any chatter between Dorian and the other ships. It was just me and the beast. "Let's keep drifting for a few minutes. Try to listen."

His grunt of agreement was enough and we floated farther away from the shuttle, from the net, from the battle taking place behind us. The wall of Hive mines seemed to mute it all. I could see flashes of light, explosions and ion blasters firing, but it was all behind a haze.

I was about to suggest we go back when I heard it, the low-level thrum I'd heard before. I twisted and yanked on the line connecting me to Angh. "There. Did you hear that?"

"Yes. It is just ahead of us."

He was right. I could feel it, too.

As if summoned, suddenly it was there. Black as tar and shaped like a strange oblong egg at least ten times the size of our shuttle, the Hive master control hub floated like a ghost in the darkness.

It was completely smooth. No nooks or crannies. No handles or doors or exhaust pipes. It was level and even as black marble. "Angh, did we bring enough…stuff?" I didn't want to use the word *explosive* just in case the Hive was somehow listening.

"I do not know, my lady." We exchanged a look and moved closer to the object. I was very sure the thing was unmanned. This was an automated system, an artificial intelligence controlled remotely by the Hive. God only knew how long this thing had been out here. Days? Months? Years?

When we were close enough to touch it, I reached into my bag and pulled out the first set of explosives, quickly attaching it to the side. They'd all been set for five minutes. When we placed the last one, or hit the main switch, the countdown would begin.

Still connected, we floated along the outside of the thing, making sure to place explosives everywhere we could reach. I ignored the battle I knew raged behind us. If we didn't take this thing down, we wouldn't just lose a few fighters and freighters, we'd lose everyone.

We'd completed a circle around the object and stopped at its apex where Angh noticed the first visible difference in the smooth exterior. He pointed to a hub that looked like a communication antenna, crystal and silver, the buzzing in my head intensified as we drew closer. "I shall place my last piece there."

I nodded and double-checked my bag. Empty. "Okay. I'm out."

We drifted closer. I bobbed around like a kite in the wind at the end of the connection as Angh used his fuel pod to pull us both toward the top of the orb. He reached into his back, drew out the final explosive, and attached it to ship, just below the crystal protruding from the tip. I shuddered with relief as the explosive locked on and a light in my helmet went red, indicating the countdown had begun.

Angh's smile looked more like a snarl as he lifted his hands from the orb and braced his legs beneath him to push us both away.

A jolt of blue lightning rose from the floating Hive hub, up his legs, encompassing his entire body. He looked like Frankenstein's Monster being brought to life.

"Angh!" I yanked on the connection between us, igniting my jet pod to separate him from the orb, pulling him behind me, dead weight, as we moved farther away. I didn't care what direction we were going, only that we were getting away from the huge-ass Hive control center.

And the massive number of explosives that were going to go off in a matter of minutes.

"Angh. Can you hear me?" My heart pounded so loudly in my ears I nearly missed his soft moan. "Angh. Wake up. Warlord, shake it off. We have to get out of here."

His hands moved and I sighed with relief. To my surprise, he unhooked me from the cord that connected us and pushed me away from him, back toward the net, and our ship. "Go, my lady. Get out of here."

"No. I'm not leaving you."

His voice sounded tired. "That blue light. It did something. My fuel pods are almost empty. I can't make it back. But you can. Go. Go now. Go to your mates. I am nothing. Leave me."

"No. God dammit, Angh. You are not going all noble on me." But it wasn't completely noble. He was right. The blast from the Hive orb had fried his fuel pods, and we were a long, long way from the shuttle. I might be able to make it back on my own. But dragging a beast? I wasn't sure.

"Go. Return to your mates."

"No." I got closer and he shoved at me with his arms, trying to force me to abandon him. "God dammit, Angh. Hold still. I'm not leaving you, and that's an order."

In the end, I had to grab the stubborn beast from behind, wrapping my arm through the straps of his fuel pod where he couldn't reach me, and fired my jet packs, gaining as much momentum as I could.

If the net didn't go down when the explosives fired, we'd fry when we tried to pass it. But if the net didn't go down, we were all doomed anyway.

The explosion was blinding. Brilliant. So hot I felt like my space armor was melting to the back of my legs, burning my flesh. I ignored the pain and kept going, fired my fuel pod until I had nothing left.

And then we drifted.

Trapped. Out of fuel. Running out of oxygen.

And the net was still there.

———

Dorian

THE BLAST ROCKED THE SMALL SHUTTLE, THE TWO PRILLON warriors shouting curses as they were tossed around like bouncing balls in the back. When they regained their feet, the eldest of the two cousins strapped himself in to the co-pilot's seat.

"Where is your mate, Dorian?"

I checked the scans and searched the screen before me. Saw nothing. "I don't know."

The comm line opened and I knew who it was before I heard Seth's voice. "Tell me Chloe wasn't in the middle of that blast."

"I don't know. We're searching for her now." I didn't need to tell him how desperate I was to find her. He could feel it.

"Keep me posted." Seth closed the link but I paid him no attention, my entire being focused on finding the only woman in the galaxy who mattered to me right now. My brave, fearless mate.

"I see something." The Prillon next to me pointed to his sensors and enlarged the screen. It was Chloe, the back of her armor charred and frayed. And she was hanging onto Angh's back, dragging him with her. Relief flooded me at the sight of her, alive.

The warlord appeared to be unconscious.

What the fuck had happened out there?

"They're still on the other side of the net."

"Can you get a reading on their life signs?" I asked. The co-pilot ran his hands over the controls, re-linking the ship's system to the armored space suits Chloe and Anghar wore.

"Anghar is critical. Oxygen low. His suit is losing pressure and his core body temperature is too low."

Fuck. "What about Chloe?" She wasn't Commander Phan at the moment. Not to me. She was mine. Chloe. My mate.

"Oxygen low. She's not as cold, but she's running out of air."

"How much time do they have left?" I asked.

He scanned the control panel. "Less than five minutes."

"I'm going after them. Either of you don't want to come along, jump in a space suit and go the other direction."

My co-pilot grunted as if insulted, and his cousin knelt on the floor behind us. "You'll have to ram the net. I will put on a flight suit and get ready to retrieve them." The Prillon warrior rose, walked to the back of the shuttle and started to put on a space suit like the ones Anghar and Chloe wore. I'd have to get him close enough to pull them in.

"We should fire at the net first," my co-pilot said. "This ship has a few weapons."

I reached for the ion blaster controls. "Brace yourselves. We're going in hot."

"Excellent." The Prillon roared behind us as I opened fire, careful to aim away from where my mate drifted, practically helpless.

The blast hit and amazingly, the hub exploded, a burst of energy traveling along previously invisible lines to the next hub...and the next. The entire net went down in a cascade of red fire and explosions of sound so loud they rocked the small shuttle. The ripple effect of each blast pushed Angjar and Chloe farther and farther away from the shuttle.

"I'm going through."

"Do it." The Prillon behind me slammed his hand down on the manual control, sealing me and the co-pilot inside as the back of the shuttle emptied of atmosphere. He was hooked to a secure point just inside the exterior doors, the cold dark of space stretched out before him as I raced toward the net.

"Contact in 3, 2, 1."

The hull of the shuttle rammed the blasted remains of one of the net's hubs. The engine strained and I pushed through until the structure shattered.

I reached for the comm even as I raced to my mate. "Commander Karter, this is Captain Kanakar."

"Go ahead, Captain." The commander's voice was clipped, all business, and I could hear the chaos of battle on the control deck of the Battleship.

"The net is down, sir. The battlegroup is clear to push through."

The sounds of cheering on the command ship reached us, but I didn't smile. Not yet. My mate was still out there.

"Understood, Captain. And Commander Phan?"

"I don't know yet, sir. We're retrieving her and Warlord Anghar now."

"Gods be with you, Captain." The line went dead and I pushed the shuttle faster, toward the small floating targets I knew were the Atlan and my mate.

We moved in close and I clenched my teeth as the Prillon warrior flew out the back of the shuttle. It felt like hours, but in reality it was only a few minutes before the

Prillon returned, pulling both Chloe and Anghar with him.

He floated them into the rear of the shuttle and closed the exterior door. It took long minutes for the chamber to regain pressure and the interior door to open. I abandoned the controls to my co-pilot as I reached Chloe's side and pulled the helmet from her head.

She blinked up at me, slowly, as if she were dazed, but she smiled. "We did it."

"Yes, love. You did. You saved us all." I knelt there and held her as the Prillon took off his suit and attended to the Atlan. We were in Hive controlled space, behind the now destroyed net, but I didn't want to take any chances. I ordered the co-pilot to get us back to the main launch bay of Battleship Karter as quickly as possible.

———

Chloe

Things were insane back on the Karter. When our small shuttle was docked, support staff helped us off, assisting in removing the excess armor and weapons.

The commander himself approached before I even unstrapped my thigh holster.

"Commander," he said. I stopped what I was doing and gave him my full attention. "Well done." He glanced to Angh and the Prillon who was assisting him with his gear.

"He needs medical, sir," I told him. Dorian stood at my side. I could feel our connection through the collar, so much more intense than the feel of his hand on my shoulder. Outwardly, he was chill. But I knew he was restraining himself for the sake of propriety.

"I do not," Angh replied, a slight grin turning up the corner of his mouth.

"Excellent work, Warlord Anghar. Now get yourself and your beast to the med unit to be seen to. That's an order."

Angh looked to me. "I owe you my life."

I shook my head. "We saved each other. I'd say we're even."

He didn't like my answer much, but nodded, then looked to the commander. He shook off the Prillon's assistance. "If I'm going to the med unit, I'll walk on my own," he grumbled. Based on that cranky tone alone, I knew he was going to be all right.

We watched his retreating form as he left the shuttle area. Others stepped out of his way. While they gave him deference because of his rank as warlord, it seemed they somehow knew he'd been the one to save us all.

"Chloe!"

I heard my name at the same time I felt the hot pulse of relief and possessiveness flood my collar. Seth.

I spun about as I was scooped up into my mate's arms, a fierce hug that practically knocked the air from my lungs.

"Captain, give the commander some space," Karter said.

Seth set me back on my feet, but didn't let me go. "With all due respect, Commander, Chloe went past the net in a fucking space suit to set charges that blew up the fucking command hub for the entire net. Once that blew, one shot from the other shuttle annihilated the whole thing. What she did was fucking insane and dangerous and if I want to hold my mate, I will."

Oh shit.

The commander was quiet as he studied Seth. I felt my mate's defiance through the collar.

"I agree," the commander finally replied. "Hold your mate. You both have earned it."

Dorian cleared his throat and Karter shook his head. "All three of you have earned it."

"What the fuck do you think you were doing, Commander Phan? Against my orders?" Bruvan's voice cut through the shuttle bay as he stomped toward us. The rest of his crew followed, but they weren't hostile, perhaps only curious.

My hackles rose at the other commander's tone. His attitude, his very existence.

Seth released me, walked over to Bruvan and punched him in the nose. I stood staring, motionless, completely surprised.

Bruvan bent at the waist, his hand on his face, swearing. Yeah, Seth had broken it, for sure, based on the sick bone crunching sound.

"Throw me in the brig, Commander. I don't give a shit," Seth said, pulling me back into him again. I could feel his rage, his harsh breathing.

"Everyone saw it. You're all witnesses. Commander, you need to—"

"Stop talking," Karter said.

Bruvan slowly stood, his hand still over his nose, blood dripping down off his chin and onto his chest armor.

"But they disobeyed orders and this captain assaulted me."

"Yes, they did and because of it the entire battlegroup isn't under Hive control. As for the assault, at least Captain Mills did it for me. It wouldn't look good if the commander of the entire battlegroup hit one of his subordinates. Or is it insubordinate?"

Bruvan's eyes narrowed as he breathed hard through his mouth.

"I heard the comms, Commander. What you told your team, how you tied the hands of the other shuttle. The recap Dorian gave to the ReCon group. All of it. You might be used to working I.C. and having everything cloaked, but not here."

I felt Dorian's hand once again on my shoulder.

"Your actions were reckless and against protocol. I am stripping you of your rank of commander here and now, but you will go before a hearing to determine penalties."

A bubble of surprise filled me. And a sense of karma. I didn't wish an entire battlegroup's lives for redemption, but it was a perk.

Bruvan started to squawk and spout crap about how the I.C. will bury all the transmissions, that nothing he did was out of the ordinary.

"Out of the ordinary? If your actions that we all witnessed is *ordinary* for you, then I will have a talk with I.C. and have your past missions unsuppressed."

Commander Karter flagged down a waiting security team. "Take Bruvan to his quarters, enhanced lock."

Within seconds, my nemesis was dragged away and I had to hope that would be the last I saw of him.

"As for you, Commander Phan."

"Sir?"

"You're dismissed. Get some sleep. Your mates have

permission to detain you in your quarters for twelve hours to do so. If I see you before then, you will be stripped of your rank as well."

Seth leaned in, his warm breath fanning my ear as he said, "Don't worry, mate, we'll strip you naked. You can keep your rank."

14

hloe, fifteen hours later...

"ARE YOU GOING TO BE OKAY?" I ASKED ANGH. WE WERE IN the transport room, but off to the side. Everyone had peeled off the heavy space suits, but most of the warriors still reeked of sweat, fear and war. They hadn't had a break like I had. But we were all here. And that was a victory that wouldn't have been possible without the huge Atlan standing before me. I knew my mates were watching me, but I couldn't see a thing around Angh's big body. He looked haggard, as if he hadn't rested at all. His armor still in place, I had no idea if he'd slept or eaten or taken a moment away from his duties since our return.

My men hadn't gone far since we'd returned from battle. In fact, all we'd done is climb into bed, hold each other and sleep. They *had* stripped me naked, all three of us were bare, but all we'd done is crash and crash hard, pulled so I was halfway over Seth's lean body, Dorian tucked into my back. I couldn't blame them for wanting to touch me because I'd felt the same need to keep them close. And now, in the transport room, even though I could sense them through the collars, even across the expanse of the battleship, I needed the reassurance of seeing them with my own eyes. Of feeling them, alive and whole.

Whatever medical attention he needed had been swift and he was ready to move on. His life wasn't here anymore. He was destined for a new life on The Colony.

Angh nodded. "Yes, Commander."

Inwardly, I rolled my eyes. "We've been through battle together. Perhaps even more than that." I lifted my hand to my head, felt relief at the relative quiet of the NPU beneath my scalp, but the buzzing was still there, an indefinable thing that would always connect me to this Atlan, to the other contaminated warriors, and to the Hive. "I think we can skip formality, Angh, don't you?"

He relaxed slightly, nodded once more. "Yes, Lady Chloe."

Well, it wasn't completely without formality, but it seemed to be the closest he could get, and I found it somewhat endearing. He wasn't one for many words, but I wanted to know he was going to be fine. "You have a chance at a second life. I've heard The Colony is a great place to live." I sounded like a Realtor on Earth trying to upsell a bad neighborhood. The words felt shallow, even to my own ears. "There have been several brides from Earth who now live there. Perhaps you will be tested for one of your own?"

His mouth fell open as if he'd never considered the possibility.

"Like this? I assure you, Commander, I mean, Lady Chloe, the testing will not find a match."

"Any female would be lucky to have you." Those words were complete truth and I would fight anyone who said otherwise. "You've earned the right to happiness. You are an excellent warlord and veteran in your own right."

"Thank you."

Commander Karter joined us, slapped Angh on the back. "The coordinates are loaded, transport is ready."

Angh offered me a slight bow, then moved to shake a few fighters' hands. He stopped in front of Seth.

"No hard feelings?" Seth asked. I felt my mate's concern for the warlord. While I hadn't been there, he'd told me that Angh had asked Seth to kill him, to end the misery of his life when Seth's ReCon team had decided to save him, to knock him out and take him off that ship. Angh had been so integrated, he'd asked for death. To die a warrior was perhaps the better outcome for some so heavily integrated by the Hive. But for Angh, the med unit was able to remove some of the integrations, but certainly not all. He could lead a full life if he chose. A mate, children, a new career within the Coalition on The Colony. He just had to want it.

"Thank you for saving my life," Angh replied. "I haven't said it before and I apologize for that. The battle has proven that I am more warlord than Hive and that I can still be an asset."

While he said the words, I wasn't sure if he truly believed them. I had to hope the others on The Colony, those who'd been through similar horrors and survived could help him in ways we never could.

"Keep in touch, Angh. That's an order." The beast actually grinned at me.

Seth put his free hand on the Atlan's upper arm, the closest thing to a man hug I was going to see on the Karter.

Angh moved down the line, saying goodbye to the others before walking up to the transport pad. Without any fanfare, he nodded and the sizzle and electrical pull made the floor vibrate, made the hairs on the back of my neck stand on end.

Within seconds, he was gone. On to a new life. Safe from the Hive and hopefully in a place where he could find peace and happiness. And if I could connect with Warden Egara, or the human women on The Colony, I might be able to do a little matchmaking, get him an Earth bride of his own. Perhaps his inner beast would force him by going into his mating fever. I'd heard of that happening before. He'd have to take a mate or he'd be executed.

The thought made me sad, and I vowed to contact the warden as soon as possible. Maybe she could pull some strings. I doubted it, but it never hurt to ask.

Seth's arm circled about my waist and pulled me from my thoughts. I turned my head to look up at him, saw the easy smile. "Ready?" he asked.

I offered a small nod and he steered me toward Dorian. Everyone, obviously, knew we were mated, but we'd agreed there would be no more PDA. We could be touchy feely and affectionate in our quarters, but that was private. That was for us alone. I loved my mates, but it wasn't professional for a commander to be making out in the corridors like a teenager. I'd give them everything when we were alone. Out here, I'd told them to hold back, and they had respected my request.

The hand on my hip was a reasonable concession and it felt good.

While we'd been asleep, Commander Karter had put out notice that all who had participated in the Battle of the Beast, as it was being called, had a three-day furlough from mission assignments, although they were expected to work on the ship.

We watched Angh disappear on the transport pad.

"Captains," Commander Karter called. My mates turned and saluted. Standing between them, I did the same. "I've given you all two days leave. The doctor doesn't feel Commander Phan is ready to return to work. Something about her neural pathways needing more time to recover."

I frowned as Dorian replied. "Why was I not told? That is unacceptable. I will discuss this with the doctor at once." He didn't seem the least bit concerned about mouthing off to the other Prillon warrior, our commander.

"Stand down, Dorian. Why do you think I'm here?"

Seth's jaw was clenched tightly, his hands in fists at his sides as he shook his head so slightly I barely noticed the action.

"Captain Mills?"

"I'm fine, Commander. But I'm not leaving her side until she has been medically cleared."

He eyed the duo, then me. "I can't blame you. Within hours of arrival, I sent your mate on a dangerous mission that nearly got her killed. I understand your need to protect her—"

"All due respect, Commander, but you don't. Not yet. Not until you have a mate of your own." Dorian stepped forward slightly, placing his hand on my arm as if he was protecting me from the commander. I expected the Prillon to take offense, but he seemed to understand the caveman maneuver, even sympathize with Dorian's primitive nature. He was a good man. A great leader. And I wondered why he didn't have a mate.

Commander Karter bowed slightly, just the slightest tilt of his hips, to me, not to my mates. "Lady Mills, based on the standard black on your collars, I see you have yet to claim these two as your mates."

I flushed hotly then. While he no doubt knew we'd fucked like rabbits that first night, the collars didn't lie about the lack of an official Prillon claiming. He knew what was required since he was Prillon himself. Seth and Dorian had to fuck me at the same time, to spill their seed in me. Only then would the collars change color and complete the match. It was like saying wedding vows, except for the fact I was going to have two cocks deep inside me. There was no going back. And unlike Earth, there was no divorce.

Seth and Dorian remained silent.

"Forty-eight hours, fighters. I don't want to see the three of you before then. I don't want reports from your supervisors telling me you've answered a mission ping. As far as I'm concerned, you're on leave. And as for your mate's role within the command center, I need her back at her post, healthy and happy, as soon as possible."

"All due respect, Commander, but I don't want my

mate going on any more missions." Seth's voice was cold as ice.

I opened my mouth to protest, but the commander beat me to it. "The Hive set one trap. There could be more. She saved the entire battlegroup. She saved your lives as well."

"Yes, sir, but that doesn't mean I want her in any further danger," Seth said. The hand about my waist tightened and he turned us around, led us out of the transport room.

"If I need her, she goes. There's only one way she sits on my bridge, Captain. You know the rules as well as I do."

"Yes, we do." That was Dorian, and he was grinning. What the hell had just happened?

"And, Captains?" We turned slightly, to look at the commander. He pointed toward us. "Get those damned collars the right color."

I'd thought I'd blushed before, but now I felt like my face was on fire. Nothing like your boss telling you to go get double penetrated by two hot, sexy mates.

Dorian flanked my other side. I felt small, sheltered and a little clueless. "What did Karter mean?" I asked.

"That he wants us to fuck you until you're well and truly claimed," Dorian said. "Until our collars turn gold." He was so calm and even-toned about it, I would have expected him to be speaking of dinner or the weather— even though there was no weather on a battleship.

I rolled my eyes and Seth saw the action, grinned. "Not that, the other thing."

Dorian nodded to someone who passed, then we

turned a corner, went down another corridor. "About you going on missions?"

"Yes," I replied, making sure he didn't go into more detail about how they were going to claim me, like who was going to take my pussy and who was going to take my ass. I didn't care which was which, and wondering what they would do was…exciting.

"As commander, Karter's hands are tied about sending the most skilled team on a mission. He'll risk any asset at his disposal to save his crew, to defeat the Hive."

"Right," I said, trying to prod him along. Why did he have to be so damned patient?

Perhaps Seth sensed my irritation, because he continued for Dorian. "There's only one thing that will make it impossible for you to be sent out again."

"And what's that?"

"If you're pregnant. They'll risk soldiers. Officers. Entire ship crews, but the Coalition never risks its children. They are the one thing every warrior here fights to protect."

I slowed at his words, but they kept going and stopped a few steps ahead of me.

"So you're going to try to get me pregnant in the next two days so I can, what? Be chained to a desk?"

Dorian walked over, tipped up my chin so I had to look into his light eyes. "That is what the commander spoke of, not what we intend. Come, we will talk about breeding you in our quarters."

I sputtered at that. "Breeding? I'm not a damn cow."

Dorian grinned and took my hand. Seth winked.

I felt their lightheartedness through the collars and realized they weren't serious.

Once we were in our quarters and the door slid closed behind us, I crossed my arms over my chest and tapped my foot. Waited. "This better be good."

"We've talked about a baby before," Seth began. He worked at the clasp of his thigh holster, took it off. "Hell, we've come deep in your pussy enough that you might be pregnant now."

My inner walls clenched at the truth of it. Shit. I hadn't been thinking about babies or anything else the first few times we'd been together, although it was always a possibility. But then, I never dreamed I'd be back out in space, on an op, risking my life again either. Desk jockey, that's what I'd expected. But now Commander Karter offered me so much more. For the first time since meeting my mates, I felt torn in two.

Dorian held up his hand as I opened my mouth to speak. "You decided when you first arrived that you were ready to make a baby."

"That was before I was called back up. Before Karter found out what I used to do."

"Exactly," Seth said, setting his ion pistol and holster on the table. "Things are different now. You're not just our mate. You have an important job, one that Karter will need on future missions. One that saves lives."

The end of that was said with almost a snarl. I sensed he wasn't happy about me going off on missions, but he didn't outright say no. Not like the two of them had when they discovered my rank and experience.

"You need to decide, Chloe, what you want. If you want to work with the commander and the I.C., then that's your call. We won't stop you."

That stopped me. My brain literally stalled. "What are

you saying? That the two of you will let me go off on top secret missions?"

"We don't want you volunteering for them, no," Seth admitted. He turned his head, looked at me straight on. "But if Karter thinks you're the best for the job at hand, then, yes. Of course, you'll go. But we won't stop fucking you. No way, sweetheart, but we'll take you right now to the med unit to get the birth control shot. We can wait until you're ready."

I flicked my gaze to Dorian, who nodded in agreement.

I'd told them I loved them. They knew it. Felt it. But now, with Seth's admission, I felt so much more. It was as if I were the Grinch and my heart grew bigger and bigger.

Tears slipped down my cheeks and I furiously wiped them away. Clearing my throat, I didn't know what to say. "I, um…yeah."

"Yes, you want the shot?" Dorian asked.

I nodded, then shook my head, not sure which to do. This was all so crazy.

"I volunteered to be a bride so I could leave Earth. I didn't fit in anymore. I didn't belong there. I had zero intention of returning to the I.C. I mean, you saw Bruvan. You can see why I had no plan or even a thought of doing so. But I'm not going to be happy gathering wool either."

Dorian looked confused by the human slang. He leaned against the table and crossed his ankles. Seth tugged out a chair, sat down. I stood before them, letting it all out. This was the right time. There weren't any more secrets to be kept—the mission had resolved that problem —and Karter had given us two days off.

"So when we first talked about having a baby, I wanted

it. Then things went crazy and to be honest, I hadn't thought about a baby—making one or having one—at all. I mean, did you think about breeding me while we were in the thick of battle?"

Seth's jaw clenched. "Besides dealing with the clusterfuck, I wanted you safe. Not just you, everyone on the mission."

"I don't know what a clusterfuck is," Dorian added. "But, no, a baby wasn't at the top of my mind. I was pretty much making sure our ship didn't get blown to bits."

"So before you fill me up with any more cum," I replied, staring at Seth and using his own words. "I think you should know what I'm thinking now."

They waited.

"I want to work with Commander Karter. I can't just sit idly by and let the Hive win, not when I can help. I want to go out on missions when Karter thinks I'm needed. Just like you, I have a job to do here. I can't do nothing. More warriors will die if I don't help. I'm not okay with that. I can't live with that."

"Do you think you would have come to this on your own if Karter hadn't figured out who you were?" Dorian asked.

I shrugged. "I don't know. Maybe. I wasn't happy on Earth. I've seen too much, done too much for the Fleet to go back to a normal life."

"What are you saying?" Seth asked.

I sighed. "I want to keep working, but I also want a baby. Now. I'll stay onboard, stick to the command deck while I'm pregnant, but when I'm fit for duty again, I want to go. But only if you'll be there for the baby. All the babies we might have. Just like Dorian is your second,

Seth, I need to know you'll both be there for our children if anything happens to me."

I felt fear and pain, frustration and love all swirled together through the collars.

"This is unorthodox," Dorian said, slowly shaking his head. I sensed his amazement. "Three Coalition fighters."

Seth stood, came over to me, tucked my hair behind my ear. His eyes met mine. "You have my word, as a father and a Coalition fighter, Dorian and I will be there for any children we might have."

Dorian moved to stand beside me. I was almost surrounded and it felt so good. "Prillon honor, mate. You have my vow as well."

Seth exhaled harshly. "I'm not keen on you heading out on a mission anytime soon. I need a little while to get used to it, to settle my nerves. So here's what we're going to do."

"Uh oh. Mr. Dominant is coming out," I joked.

He grinned, but his voice deepened into that tone that made my panties wet and my nipples harden. "We're going to fuck you, sweetheart, for the next two days. By the time you head back to the commend deck, you'll be setting off all the med sensors."

I laughed at that. "Cocky, much?"

"Speaking of cocks," he replied and I rolled my eyes.

"You want a baby, mate, we'll give you one. But first," Dorian lifted a hand to my collar. "I want this to be golden. I need to claim you, to make our bond official and unbreakable. I need you, Chloe." He took my chin between his fingers and turned my head so I had to look up at him. "While Seth is your primary mate, the collars, the claiming, is my custom." Dorian glanced at Seth who gave him a quick nod to continue. "Do you accept Seth's claim, mate? Do you give yourself to him and me as your second freely, or do you wish to choose another primary mate?"

They looked to me with a hint of vulnerability. This was the moment I could destroy our bond. Sever it. I could deny the match. Refuse Seth and I'd be matched to another. I didn't want that and ruled it out immediately. It had been instantaneous, the connection. I wanted it to be stronger, not gone.

"Seth, if we were on Earth, I'd say I do and you'd give me a gorgeous ring. But we're not on Earth and I'd probably cut someone with a big rock on my finger. Neither is me. I'm here with you, between you both, because I am proud to accept both of you as my mates. There is no second. Only the two of you. Mine."

Dorian's hand cupped my hip, squeezed. "I claim you in the rite of naming. You are mine and I shall kill any other warrior who dares touch you."

"I agree," Seth added. "I'm one possessive fucker and no one will harm you. Touch you. Even look your way with desire."

I couldn't help but smile, knew this moment was the closest thing to a wedding I was going to get. I stood before them in my uniform, all black, but no armor. Since I wasn't going on a mission, it hadn't been necessary.

"So how does this work? The, um, claiming?"

The men's gazes went all primitive and hot.

"We fuck you together," Dorian said. "As primary mate, Seth will choose which tight hole he wants to claim."

Seth's hands moved to the hem of my shirt and started to tug it up. "She just said there's no primary mate."

"Aren't you the Dominant here?" Dorian asked, brow raised. "Then act like it."

Seth's casual stance, his easy smile, slipped. He stepped back, leaving me with my shirt bunched up beneath my arms.

"Dorian's right," Seth said, his voice clear. He pointed to the entry. "Behind that door, I'm in charge. Strip, mate. Show us what belongs to us."

Oh yeah, there was the version of Seth that got me all hot and bothered. I licked my suddenly dry lips as Dorian stepped back and moved to lean against the table again. He crossed his arms over his chest, watchful. Seth might be in charge, but Dorian got off on watching me submit.

I finished working my shirt off, let it slip from my fingers and fall to the floor. Seth just twirled his finger in the air to indicate that I continue, but his gaze roved over the bare skin I was slowly exposing.

Only when I was finally naked did they move. And when they did, I found myself tossed over Seth's shoulder and carried to the bed where I was unceremoniously dropped on it. I bounced up and I scrambled to my knees.

"Ah, just where we want you." Seth began to undo the front of his pants, Dorian not far behind.

With their cocks out—the rest of them completely covered in their uniforms—it reminded me of my place, at least here in bed. I was the one who took the commands, who did what I was told without question. And without words, I knew exactly what they expected. Shuffling forward, I bent down and gripped Dorian's cock with my fist as I took Seth's into my mouth. They both groaned as I began to work them, Dorian as I slid my snug grip up and down, collecting his pre-cum with a swipe of my thumb, and Seth as I swirled my tongue over the flared crown.

"Good girl, Chloe. Get us ready to claim you."

I didn't stop, but based on the fact that they were like steel beams in my hand and mouth, I had to question how much more ready they needed to be.

After a minute, I switched, taking Dorian as deep as I could as I worked Seth's cock, my saliva making my grip slide so well. They felt differently against my tongue, tasted differently and I loved both their flavors. I had no idea they each had their own fucking style.

"Enough," Dorian growled, tugging gently on my hair to pull me off of him. "Turn around, on hands and knees."

I licked my lips, glanced up at them through my lashes, saw their cheeks flushed, their muscles tense. Their eyes were darker, heated, predatory. And I was their prey. Turning slowly, I settled into the position they wanted. I knew, when I heard not a sound, not even breathing, that they were staring at my upturned bottom. With my knees parted as they'd instructed before, my pussy and trained ass were completely exposed.

"You've taken the training plugs, mate, and we've opened that ass up for our cocks. But none of the plugs are as big as we are. It's going to be a tight fit." Dorian only stated fact, one that I already knew, I'd mentally prepared for.

I clenched my inner muscles at the thought. The first day I was here, we'd fucked and their cocks had stretched my pussy. I knew it was going to be hard going with a cock going deep into my ass. And it wasn't just that, I'd have a second one in my pussy as well.

"I'm ready," I breathed, wiggling my hips.

I felt the slide of a finger over my slick folds. "Yes, we can see that you are," Seth added. "While your pussy's dripping wet, we need to get this virgin ass all slick too. We don't want to hurt you."

The slick lube was coated over my tight opening. Fingers began to circle and press, working it in. More was collected, added as my body opened for the tip of it to enter, to spread the cool gel. At the same time one of my mates was preparing my ass, the other reached around and cupped my breasts, played with them, tugged and pinched my nipples.

It wasn't long before I was squirming, shifting my hips to take more of the fingertip in my ass. I was ready for more.

I didn't have to say anything, but a cock nudged my pussy and slid in deep, as if it knew exactly where it wanted to be. Deep inside of me.

I tossed my head back and moaned. I recognized the cock as Seth's. He was more demanding, rougher in his fucking. And his thumb slid in even deeper so I was penetrated in both holes.

"Almost ready, sweetheart."

He wasn't planning on staying in my pussy. I knew he'd be the one to fuck my ass for the claiming. He was just warming me up, making me as hot and close to orgasm as I could be before they both worked their way into me.

I'd been right. Within a minute, Seth pulled completely from my body and Dorian stopped playing with my breasts. Dorian tugged his shirt over his head, pushed his pants down over his hips and moved to sprawl across the bed, his knees bent and his feet touching the floor.

"Crawl on over here, mate." His head was turned and his pale eyes met mine. He was ready. The way his cock pointed toward the ceiling, long and thick, I imagined all of it deep inside me. The quick warm-up of Seth's cock only made me needier than ever. I carefully climbed over him, eager to straddle his lean hips. Lifting up, I got his cock beneath me, right where it wanted to be.

I looked to Seth, knowing he was in charge.

"That's a good girl. Take him deep. Fuck him. Ride him until you're almost ready to come. Then stop."

I whimpered at the last, knowing it was impossible to stop the pleasure of being with both of them once we got going.

"You'll stop before you come, sweetheart, or we'll spank your ass before we claim you."

I whimpered, thinking maybe that wasn't such a bad idea.

Dorian groaned. "Shit, she likes that idea."

Seth grinned. "She does. We'll have to try that another time. Don't worry, we'll spank you all you want. Later. But now, we're claiming you."

Dorian took hold of my hips, pulled me down onto him in one long, deep stroke until I was sitting upon his thighs again.

I gasped at being filled, relieved that there was something deep inside me once again. Dorian groaned, his fingers clenched. He pushed up, then lowered me again, fucking me as he wanted. He'd been more than ready to claim me, sweat dotted his brow and his jaw was clenched tight. Every time he took a breath, his nostrils flared.

Out of the corner of my eye, I could see Seth stripping

out of his clothes, coating his cock in the lube. But I didn't pay him any mind; Dorian and his bold handling had all my focus.

When I felt Seth's hand on my shoulder, Dorian stilled, his cock embedded deep. He pulled me down to kiss me, our bodies touching, my breasts pressed firmly against his hard chest.

Seth's cock nudged my entrance next. He'd prepared me well, for I was slick and my tight ring of muscle prepared for an object to pass. But it had never had a cock, not something of Seth's girth.

I whimpered against Dorian's mouth as he continued to kiss me while Seth nudged and pressed, coaxed my body to flower open for him. It didn't take long, for somehow I knew this was what I wanted. My mind and body relented, gave over to Seth, for he wasn't going to stop. Oh, I could tell him no and, of course, he'd leave my ass untouched. But his dominance was what I wanted. This was the ultimate submission.

Between them, I felt perfectly safe and yet completely vulnerable. I was exposed, accepting something in a way that was so taboo on our home planet. Yet here with my mates, it was perfect. It was exactly what the three of us needed to do to prove to ourselves we were safe, whole, together. That we were one and that I was the one to join us. My body might be what connected us physically, but the collars linked our minds.

And as Seth's cock popped into my ass, settled for a moment to allow me to adjust before he began to work his way deeper and deeper into me, I was theirs. Completely. Totally.

Once Seth was in to the hilt, they began to move. Our

breaths were loud in the room, the slick slide of cocks my sole focus.

I could do nothing. I couldn't move, couldn't think. Could only feel as they filled me to the brink of pain, yet not any further. They gave me everything I needed and then some. More than I ever imagined.

And when I came, I couldn't hold back, the pleasure too great. The collars made me sense their pleasure too. I knew how much they liked being in me at the same time, how tight it was, how incredible the bond that joined us.

It swirled and escalated, grew and then exploded. I screamed, unable to hold anything back. They rocked and stroked me deep with their cocks before they, too, came. I felt the hot pulses of their seed deep inside me as the collar about my neck heated.

I knew, without seeing it, that the collar was now golden. The claim was official. I had their cocks, their cum, their hearts. All of them.

And with them deep inside me, they knew they had all of me too.

I might be a commander in my own right, but between my mates, I was just Chloe Phan. No, I was Lady Mills. They'd fought for me. Not only the Hive, Commander Karter, but even me.

But now, I'd submitted. There was no longer a fight. I was once and for all, their mate.

EPILOGUE

S eth, Nineteen Months Later

IT HAD BEEN A LONG, EXHAUSTING DAY. THE MISSION HAD pulled me from bed. Those were the comm pings I hated the most. The ones where I had Chloe pressed to my front, like two spoons in a drawer. My arm was slung over her, my palm settled perfectly so it cupped her breast. It was the same position we always slept unless Dorian grabbed her first. Then he was on his back and he practically had Chloe tucked into his side. She could sleep either way; she was used to her mates constant need to touch and hold her.

Often, I'd wake her by sliding my cock into her sweet pussy from behind, fucking her slowly until she awakened with an orgasm, and my cum deep inside her. With Dorian, all he had to do was lift her up so knees straddled his hips and she was riding him.

Ever since the Battle of the Beast, over a year and a half ago, where we nearly lost her, we'd become unbelievably close. I thought I'd been in love with her before, but after seeing her save us all, risk everything to protect not just the entire battlegroup and one wounded beast, I couldn't look at her without something breaking inside.

I loved her so much it hurt, the pain one I welcomed, protected and cherished like a fragile, delicate treasure. Because as strong as Chloe was, that's what she was to me. My life. My soul. Fragile and beautiful and perfect. The intensity of the bond could have been due to the claiming that occurred a few days later, when Dorian and I claimed her for the first time together, our bond complete, the claiming official. The day she became ours forever and our collars changed to gold.

I didn't really give a fuck as to the reason. It didn't matter. Chloe was ours and we never stopped showing her. I shucked my uniform and left it in a pile at my feet as I hopped into the shower tube to wash away the grime, the insanity of the mission. Putting one hand on the clear wall, I sighed, thinking of Chloe and how we'd taken her. Both she and Dorian had heard the comms ping, giving me a fifteen-minute warning to join my group for debriefing.

"I must have you, mate, before I go," I'd said, my voice deep and rough from sleep, my cock hard as a fucking rail. There was no way I could meet the team with a lead pipe in my pants.

She'd lifted her head off Dorian's arm; she'd used him as a pillow, and smiled sleepily. Dorian had growled, lifted her carefully onto his lap and slipped inside. I'd grabbed the lube and coated myself liberally, taking a little time to prepare my mate first with my fingers as Dorian warmed her up. Only when she was panting and writhing on Dorian's cock, her ass clenching and milking my digits to go deeper did I work my way past that tight ring of muscle and fuck her deep. It wasn't easy, even after all this time, but she took both of us beautifully. The ATB was still put to use, especially for play. But this morning, all she got was cock, for I'd needed to be close to my mate, to feel the connection between us through the collars before I went off on my mission.

And now, I wanted her again. But I would have to collect her from her post on the command deck and, like usual, I couldn't walk about with a hard dick. So I gripped the base and stroked myself to completion. It was a waste of perfectly good cum, liking it best when I planted it deep inside Chloe, but the lingering adrenaline from battle forced my hand. Literally.

Dressing quickly in a clean uniform, I double timed it to the command deck, eager for my mate. The door slid open and there she was, sitting at her assigned spot, special I.C. headpiece over the side of her head. To say that made her look all commanding and sexy was an understatement. Here, she was in charge, or almost in charge, and that was hot as fuck. Just as hot as when she stripped bare just inside the entry of our quarters after a long day, dropped to her knees in submission and asked for our cocks.

Sensing my presence, she spun around in her chair and smiled. "There's my girl," I said low, really more for me than anyone else.

"You're back," she said, stating the obvious.

"Just."

"I know you weren't thrilled about the idea of me going on missions, but this is ridiculous. I can't actually get up."

She was grinning and running a hand over her big belly. She was so big with our child in her womb that she looked like she had a watermelon beneath her modified black uniform shirt. She was glowing, radiant even, her hair pulled back in a simple ponytail. She was so gorgeous, so lush and ripe I got hard all over again. Good thing she was horny as fuck when pregnant.

I walked over to her, took her hands in mine and tugged her to standing.

"How's our little man?" I asked, placing my palm over her belly. She took my hand, slid it down lower and I felt a thump. A kick or an elbow.

"That is a little gymnast and I think she's going to doing a somersault right out of me."

We'd had this debate of boy versus girl since the very beginning. Neither of us wanted to know the sex. Perhaps it was our Earth upbringing where it was fairly easy to avoid the answer. But Dorian was almost frantic with his interest in knowing what we'd planted in her belly. He swore it was a golden-eyed girl, and I had a sneaking suspicion that he was right.

"We're in big trouble if this basketball is a girl."

Chloe removed her special headpiece, set it carefully in its case and looked toward the commander's office.

I gave Karter a slight nod of greeting.

"Commander, I'll take that into Karter for you." An ensign held a hand out. Chloe handed it off and looked to

Karter to make sure he knew about the hand-off. They'd been particular as fuck about that little piece of equipment. It—no, Chloe—had saved many lives with it and no one wanted to see it damaged. Karter was responsible for the headpiece and I was responsible for the wearer.

"Let's go find Dorian and get you off your feet."

"God, yes. I haven't seen them in two weeks and I'm starving."

I heard her discontent but didn't feel it through the collars. She was just as excited about this baby as we were.

I headed in the direction of the main cafeteria, knowing Dorian would be there this time of day for an early meal. When we entered, we saw him easily enough. It was hard to miss the big Prillon warrior sitting beside a high chair and a one-year old little girl smacking a small spoon against her tray.

Warriors all around smiled and were happier having her about. She wasn't the only infant on the ship, but she was the only one who had two captains and a commander as parents.

Dorian stood, came over to Chloe and kissed her as I took his spot beside Dara. She was the light of all our lives and the moment she was born, Dorian and I were completely and utterly destroyed.

Having a female mate was one thing, but a baby? We were doomed. Obsessive? In love? Definitely. But if we thought we were possessive and protective of her mother, we were wrong. We took Dara's safety and happiness to an extreme that had all warriors laughing at us.

As if I gave a shit.

Nothing in my life had gone according to plan, and I'd never been so grateful. I had absolutely every fucking thing I ever wanted and pushed away. And soon, very soon, we'd have another baby. Dorian was probably right. The little acrobat in her belly was probably another girl and we were going to be in even more trouble. Our girls owned us, and we didn't want it any other way.

It was becoming harder and harder to leave our girls for missions. Dorian and I had talked about it. Retiring. Giving up Coalition life for a peaceful existence on Prillon Prime. A battleship wasn't the place to raise a family.

Chloe was happy in her job, but she'd been the one to ignore the doctor's recommendation for birth control for a few months before having a second child. No, she'd gotten pregnant almost right away after her recovery. Sure, we were virile mates and we'd certainly filled up that perfect pussy with enough cum to make a dozen babies, but only one mattered. And it was in her now, just a few more days until it was going to make its presence very known.

Dorian helped Chloe settle into a chair and Dara clapped and blew air kisses at her mother.

"Good day?" Dorian asked. He'd retired the week after Dara was born. He'd walked into his supervisor's office and turned in his papers. He was the stay-at-home dad. The big Prillon, the fierce pilot and warrior who stood almost eight-feet tall, was the primary caregiver of a newborn baby. Once she'd stopped nursing, he took her everywhere with him. I'd returned to ReCon 3 and Chloe had gone back to work for the commander after her leave.

Listening to the Hive. Helping Battlegroup Karter take back three planets in this sector, a level of advancement and victory that hadn't been seen in this sector in decades.

It had gone well, our arrangement, but now I felt what Dorian had. I wanted to be there for this baby. I didn't need to fight anymore. It was time for younger, wilder fighters to take over.

"We wanted to ask you something, mate," Dorian said, waving for someone to bring a plate of the evening's meal to Chloe.

"Oh?" she asked, playing peek-a-boo with Dara.

"How would you feel about spending some time on Prillon Prime?"

"It would be nice for Dara and the acrobat to meet her grandparents."

Dorian's family lived there and had met Dara once, but only for a few days. My family, the only family I had left, was my sister, Sarah, and she lived on Atlan with her huge brute of a mate, a beast named Nyko. My brothers were dead, killed by the Hive. My parents? Long gone. This family, my family, was the only thing left in the universe I cared about.

I glanced at Dorian, then Chloe. "We were thinking, if you agreed, we'd move there."

An ensign brought a plate of pot roast and mashed potatoes for me and Chloe. An Earth specialty that everyone seemed to love.

"To Prillon Prime?" she asked, picking up her fork.

"Yes." Dorian's voice was even, but I sensed his hesitation. We didn't need to make Chloe upset at this late stage of her pregnancy.

"I thought you'd never ask."

Dorian and I stared at her as if she'd grown a second head instead of a baby in her belly. Dara clapped her hands with glee, for what, I had no idea. That was the joy of being one. And perfect, just like her mother with her dark hair and green eyes.

"You mean, you've wanted to move?"

"A battleship is no place to raise kids."

I glanced at Dorian and he shrugged.

"That's what we thought, but we weren't sure if you—"

"What? Wanted to retire?"

"Well, yes," I replied carefully. "I'm ready. I'm tired of fighting. I've done my time. We can't go back to Earth, but I don't want to. Dorian can relocate us to a place near his family on the Prillon home world. We can start a new life."

"Okay." Chloe dropped a bombshell on us without blinking. "I already spoke to Commander Karter about relocating. He spoke to the I.C. and I can transfer to a command base on Prillon Prime whenever we're ready." She batted her eyelashes at us. "I've been waiting on you two. I've been ready for months."

"You spoke to Karter?" Dorian asked. Our mate smiled, that secretive, feminine smile that made me crazy, and I felt my cock growing hard once more.

"I can't stop thinking about the danger to our family. To Dara. When Seth goes out on a mission. I think it will be twice as bad when this one's born." She rubbed a hand on the side of her belly. "Commander Karter told me you two will most likely be assigned to a warrior training center in the capital city. That's where the main military command base is. And another human woman, the queen, is there as well? Jessica? And they have a child, too. Someone for Dara and our new baby to be friends with."

Dorian looked as shocked as I felt. Our mate had organized our life, changed everything, and had simply been waiting for us to be done fighting. If she'd demanded I leave six months ago, I would have brushed her thoughts aside and gone on and on about the war and my duty, about protecting Earth and the other planets.

But I'd done my time. Sacrificed years of my life and both of my brothers to fighting the Hive. I was tired, not my body, but my soul. Every time I looked at Dara's joy-filled little face, her innocent eyes, it was harder and harder to leave her and go back out there. Into the dark. And death. And killing. I was so tired of killing.

Now, the only duty I felt was to her. To Dara. To the little one growing in Chloe's womb. Dorian was sure the second child would be born with golden eyes and hair, his genetic offspring. I couldn't wait to see what the little one looked like, the newest member of our family. A new innocent life to protect and love.

Chloe smiled and lifted a bite of mashed potatoes to her lips with a grin still tilting her lips. "The Fleet can send intel to Prillon Prime, whatever communications they need me to listen to and decipher. Anything I need to do, I can do from there. And they are expanding the program, recruiting more codebreakers, so I won't have to work as many hours. Since Prime Nial has a human mate, Commander Karter explained my situation to him." She rubbed her belly again and smiled at Dara. "He understood. He said I can work part time, basically set my own hours. The success we've had in this sector was the proof Doctor Helion needed to get approval from the Prime to bring more warriors into the program."

"Oh, um, okay then," I said, not sure what else to say. I forked up a bite of meat, chewed and swallowed. Holy shit. Why did I feel like I'd just been hit with a sledgehammer? I was ready for a fight, ready to cajole her, convince her to leave this ship. Beg her. Seduce her. Whatever it took. And she'd been ready to leave for months.

Probably since little Dara was born.

"That was easy," Dorian said, laughing. "Our brilliant mate is one step ahead of us, Seth."

"Keeping secrets, Chloe. I think we'll have to spank you for that."

My mate, my sexy, defiant mate threw her head back and laughed, Dara giggling with her, copying her mother out of pure joy. "You ain't seen nothing yet, boys. Wait until you're surrounded by smart, sassy women. I intend to have six or eight daughters to drive you two crazy."

Dorian leaned down and kissed her swollen belly, where I suspected another beautiful daughter grew strong. "Based on the way we can't keep our hands off each other, your prediction may come true soon enough."

My cock swelled beneath the table. A house full of children. Boy or girl, made no difference to me. They'd be loved. Protected. And our smiling mate, happy and content, would be far away from this Battleship, from the Hive, and the danger we had all lived with since the claiming.

"Promises, promises," I said. "And what if I told you I want a house full of children? A dozen, at least?"

Dorian lifted his head, in complete agreement as

Chloe buried her fingers in his hair, loving him, petting him, right there at the table.

The love coming through the collars from all three of us was so strong my eyes burned, my throat closed and the ache of loving her filled me with the sweetest pain. She leaned forward so she could speak just to me over Dorian's head. "If we eat quickly, do you think you two can take me like you did this morning?"

While her words made me want to toss her—carefully —onto the table and fuck her, I swallowed hard. "Sweetheart, you're topping from the bottom."

She had the submissive grace to turn her eyes down and blush, but then she tipped up her chin and met my gaze with her sharp green one. "Captain, I'm nine months pregnant. If I want to be fucked by both my mates, then that's what's going to happen. Never, ever argue with a pregnant woman."

Commander Karter came in then, bent down and blew raspberries on Dara's chubby cheek. Her squeal of laughter drew a dozen looks, most from the Atlan beasts who seemed to hover near my mate any time she wandered the ship. They all knew what she'd done for Warlord Anghar, and she'd earned the loyalty and protection of every beast on the ship.

And so had our daughter. Which was just fine with me.

The commander allowed little Dara to grab his hair and tug, hard, his smile at her antics rare to see. He spoke to us as he gently untangled the baby's fingers from his head. "Captains, I think you need to listen to Commander Phan and obey her orders. And while you tend to that important mission, you can let Uncle Karter take care of Dara."

Karter had become a pseudo-uncle to Dara, babysitting and becoming a baby-talking fool whenever she was around. No one said a word. They didn't dare.

But Karter's next words caused all three of us to pause. "And when that's done, I need to see all three of you in my office. The I.C. just send me some new information. I'm afraid retirement may not be an option. We'll discuss things tomorrow."

"So be it," Chloe said. The look our mate was giving us told me we were in for one hell of a ride tonight. She wanted a hard fuck and we were the only ones who could give it to her.

Dorian and I stood. "Yes, ma'am," we said with all seriousness. Where Chloe went, we went, whether that meant life on a Battleship or halfway across the galaxy on a strange, new planet.

I took her hand, helped her up and after kissing Dara on the head—who was completely oblivious of her parents because her Uncle Karter was making funny faces and sounds—we led her out of the cafeteria and toward our quarters.

"You're in charge, mate," Dorian said. "We're at your command."

"That's right. We're all yours," I agreed. It was nothing less than the truth. She owned us both. Body and soul. With the collars connecting us, there was no hiding our need for her. Our devotion had only deepened with time.

The door to our quarters slid open. She turned on her heel, bumping her belly into me as she did so, Dorian right next to me with an eager grin on his face. We both loved it when Chloe was in this kind of mood. Wild. Sexy.

Demanding.

It made her ultimate surrender all the sweeter.

She grabbed the front of each of our shirts and tugged. "That's right. You're all mine. And I want you both. Right now."

The door slid closed behind us, and we gave our mate exactly what she needed. All night long.

A SPECIAL THANK YOU TO MY READERS...

Want more? I've got **hidden** bonus content on my web site *exclusively* for those on my mailing list.

If you are already on my email list, you don't need to do a thing! Simply scroll to the bottom of my newsletter emails and click on the **super-secret** link.

Not a member? What are you waiting for? In addition to ALL of my bonus content (great new stuff will be added regularly) you will be the first to hear about my newest release the second it hits the stores—AND you will get a free book as a special welcome gift.

Sign up now! http://freescifiromance.com

FIND YOUR INTERSTELLAR MATCH!

YOUR mate is out there. Take the test today and discover your perfect match. Are you ready for a sexy alien mate (or two)?

VOLUNTEER NOW!

interstellarbridesprogram.com

DO YOU LOVE AUDIOBOOKS?

Grace Goodwin's books are now available as
audiobooks...everywhere.

LET'S TALK SPOILER ROOM!

Interested in joining my **Sci-Fi Squad**? Meet new like-minded sci-fi romance fanatics and chat with Grace! Get excerpts, cover reveals and sneak peeks before anyone else. Be part of a private Facebook group that shares pictures and fun news! Join here:

https://www.facebook.com/groups/scifisquad/

***

Want to talk about Grace Goodwin books with others? Join the **SPOILER ROOM** and spoil away! Your GG BFFs are waiting! (And so is Grace)

Join here:

https://www.facebook.com/groups/ggspoilerroom/

GET A FREE BOOK!

JOIN MY MAILING LIST TO BE THE FIRST TO KNOW OF NEW RELEASES, FREE BOOKS, SPECIAL PRICES AND OTHER AUTHOR GIVEAWAYS.

http://freescifiromance.com

ALSO BY GRACE GOODWIN

Interstellar Brides® Program

Mastered by Her Mates

Assigned a Mate

Mated to the Warriors

Claimed by Her Mates

Taken by Her Mates

Mated to the Beast

Tamed by the Beast

Mated to the Vikens

Her Mate's Secret Baby

Mating Fever

Her Viken Mates

Fighting For Their Mate

Her Rogue Mates

Claimed By The Vikens

The Commanders' Mate

Matched and Mated

Hunted

Viken Command

The Rebel and the Rogue

Interstellar Brides® Program: The Colony

Surrender to the Cyborgs

Mated to the Cyborgs

Cyborg Seduction

Her Cyborg Beast

Cyborg Fever

Rogue Cyborg

Cyborg's Secret Baby

Her Cyborg Warriors

Interstellar Brides® Program: The Virgins

The Alien's Mate

Claiming His Virgin

His Virgin Mate

His Virgin Bride

Interstellar Brides® Program: Ascension Saga

Ascension Saga, book 1

Ascension Saga, book 2

Ascension Saga, book 3

Trinity: Ascension Saga - Volume 1

Ascension Saga, book 4

Ascension Saga, book 5

Ascension Saga, book 6

Faith: Ascension Saga - Volume 2

Ascension Saga, book 7

Ascension Saga, book 8

Ascension Saga, book 9

Destiny: Ascension Saga - Volume 3

ABOUT GRACE

Grace Goodwin is a USA Today and international bestselling author of Sci-Fi and Paranormal romance with more than one million books sold. Grace's titles are available worldwide in multiple languages in ebook, print and audio formats. Two best friends, one left-brained, the other right-brained, make up the award-winning writing duo that is Grace Goodwin.

They are both mothers, escape room enthusiasts, avid readers and intrepid defenders of their preferred beverages. (There may or may not be an ongoing tea vs. coffee war occurring during their daily communications.) Grace loves to hear from readers!

All of Grace's books can be read as sexy, stand-alone adventures. But be careful, she likes her heroes hot and her love scenes hotter. You have been warned...

www.gracegoodwin.com
gracegoodwinauthor@gmail.com

Lightning Source UK Ltd.
Milton Keynes UK
UKHW021433030321
379713UK00008B/2165